Son of Orbiting Death Ray Platform

by Dr. Heinrich Heildmon

Outskirts Press, Inc.
Denver, Colorado

Son of Orbiting Death Ray Platform
By Dr. Heinrich Heildmon
Written by Michael Stork

Outskirts Press
http://www.outskirtspress.com

ISBN: 1-932672-06-0

Printed in the United States of America

Foreward by Mark Twain

What you are about to read is, at its very best, disturbing. Many times it will shock or disgust you to the point of vomiting or spontaneous bowel evacuation. Sometimes the observations are so absolutely stupid you will want to shove a sharp stick into your eye just to see any kind of point at all. But just like peeling away the layers of an onion, the deeper you look into the stories for their meaning, the less you have left over when you are done.

The author was probably kicked in the head by a horse as a child or at least should have been. He should be the poster child for abortion in the 35th year of pregnancy. Son of Orbiting Death-Ray Platform is chock-full of crap and I was insulted to have been asked to write the forward. So much so that some night, when the so-called author is sleeping, I will sneak into his mobile home and light him and everything I can find on fire and then take a big steaming dump on the ashes.

He is so stupid he probably won't even read this before the book is published.

What an idiot.

Introduction
Bare Naked and Late for Class

My very good friend Art Carter told me that life is kind of like a bucket. The bucket is empty, but it's not sad that it's empty. It is an opportunity with limitless possibilities. The bucket looks at the situation like, "Hey, what can I put in me?" I have another friend with the same outlook on life, but he seems to spend a lot of time in the emergency room having a doctor take it back out.

My personal outlook on life changes from day to day depending on how things are going at the time. For example, today my personal philosophy is, "If you pick at it, it will never heal." I also believe strongly, "You can never, and I mean NEVER, have too many napkins."

The real story of my life philosophy starts with my birth in a small town deep inside of the Forced Boredom colony in the Northwestern tip of Southeast Eucalyptus. Shortly after that, I began my never ending search for the true meaning of ambiguity. My mother and father begged me to end my quest, but I was far too young to understand English. One day while I was drinking my milk, my attention was suddenly drawn to a vision standing in the doorway. Startled by this vision, I quickly stood up and knocked my glass of milk to the floor. As if it were in slow motion, I watched the half-full glass of milk, decorated with a strange cartoon pig, crash to the floor. My mother turned and gasped as if she had just seen a half-full glass of milk, decorated with a strange cartoon pig on it, crash to the floor.

I tried to explain to my mother what had happened, but, alas, it would do no good. At that point my mother told me something, and to this very day it truly is how I live my life. She said, "Well, I guess we can't have anything nice." Oh, how right she was. Later that evening, when my father came home from working in the salt mines, he also gave me some words to live by. He said "Son, when life hands you lemons, put the lemons in a box filled with scorpions and mail it back to the bastard."

I guess Art Carter is right. Life is full of opportunities, limitless possibilities. Life really is like a bucket. And it can be filled with whatever you choose, even lemons or scorpions. I, however, choose to fill my life's bucket with napkins, because you can never have too many napkins.

Chapter 1
Son of Orbiting Death Ray Platform

I know this evil mad doctor whose life long dream (not unlike my own) is to build a legion of giant killer robots and loose them on the world. The final component to his giant killer robots is a device called a Fragulator, but sadly this Fragulator technology is incompatible with the current Spankulator technology used by makers of giant killer robot kits.

The doctor's name is be spelled G-e-o-f-f, but pronounced Roger. He has a cat named Mr.Scratches that wants people to think he thinks he is a person, but really thinks he is a cat who can fool humans into thinking he thinks he is a person. But everyone sees right through this act.

Now Dr. Geoff (Roger) is not really a mad doctor; he is just very, very angry. And he is not really evil, but his cat is. As he would explain it, "Just because I want to loose my legion of giant killer robots on the world does not make me evil." (He thinks he is more misunderstood than evil.)

Dr. Geoff (Roger) also has a dog named Bitey. Now Bitey is a good dog except for the biting part and the disturbingly large bowel movements. He is mostly a good dog.

One day Dr.Geoff (Roger) actually developed a way to integrate the Fragulator processing unit with the Spankulator body housing. He was just about to begin assembling his giant killer robots when the phone rang. I think it was probably his mom. As soon as Dr.Geoff (Roger) left, Mr. Scratches, being evil, started taunting Bitey with this new Fragulator/Spankulator interface. Now, Bitey is mostly a good dog, but he can only take so much, and he bit it.

The next morning Dr. Geoff (Roger) had found the device, but sadly the technology would be lost. Not because it had been bitten, but rather, it was embedded deep inside one of Bitey's disturbingly large bowel movements. Dr. Geoff (Roger)'s response was, “Can't use it now; 's got poop on it.”

Chapter 1
Hello Dali

I finally got hired at Lingo-Tec. As you remember, Lingo-Tec is the third largest developer of business-related acronyms and technical sounding words. They spent tens of dollars developing such technical sounding words like "poly-goodarific," "hypergoodalistic," and my favorite "scrumdilly-ishfullness."

My very good friend Winki Nudges works just down the hall from my cube-ette in the Un-Non-Food-Related Double-Negatives Department. She was working on a word to describe the pie you could have had but probably wouldn't have even if someone could have baked it for you. It was something like "un-circumstantial non-piefulness."

Just then Chucky Fluffenberg came into my cube-ette. Chucky mostly liked coming to work dressed as "Kicky the Clown." Kicky's way of bringing humor was a good old fashion kick to the groin. Along with this kicking thing, Chucky would try to rhyme everyone's name. He would try... and he would fail.

Before Kicky could tell me his "joke," Winki stopped by and informed Kicky that the boss, Les Tocmorework, wanted to see him in his office. Kicky spouted a quick rhyme of Winki's name but made a serious oversight. He completely missed the most devastating "Stinky Winki" rhyme and went for the less damaging "Hinky Winki." Now Winki, being a seasoned wordsmith, delivered a response to be revered as a classic to this day. "Maybe a nice friendly face-punching might move your ass, Chucky!"

Chapter 1

My new job at Lingo-Tec is working out great. As you know, Lingo-Tec is the third largest developer of business related acronyms and technical sounding words and phrases. My very good friend Art Carter works down the hall in the Commonly Repeated Acronym Program, also called CRAP. He is working on an acronym for "Wide-Angle Neutron Gatherer" but is having some trouble not giggling when his project comes up at the staff meetings.

My latest project is to come up with a name for a new hi-tech pair of pants. The fabric is made of the highest quality Kott-un™ (a 100% synthetic fiber made from Petrol-Eum™ and Salmonella Jeff's Zesty Mayo Drink Mix™) and a mysterious non-sticking space-age material known only as "Monkey Urine™." They have a microchip planted in the pocket that, when activated, compels the wearer to take part in any pre-specified activity. I think I am going to go with "Partici-Pants." My boss, Mr. Les Tocmorework, didn't like my first idea: "Action-Trousers." I still have a lot to learn.

Chapter 1

My very good friend, Angry Dave, is working on a new invention. As you know, that's what Angry Dave does: invents things. He is convinced that the general public wants, no, needs his new device. He calls it the "Name Detector." Basically it is a pointer that teachers use to show you where Omaha is on a map. I tell Angry Dave this very fact, and he explains, "That just proves it works." He tells me that his "Name Detector" is over 97% accurate at locating things with names. In order to improve the accuracy of the Name Detector, Angry Dave is installing a Pronoun setting, so instead of detecting "a birthday cake," it finds "that" or "him." I talked him out of installing the Attack setting. For some reason, in Attack mode, the Name Detector could only seem to find things named "eye" and "crotch."

On a far less interesting topic, my very good friend has finished his work on the "Automatic Hurt Maker." Actually, this is just a modified version of his "Automatic Welt Maker." As you remember, the Automatic Welt Maker consists of two main components: a 24-inch metal ruler and Angry Dave smacking you with it. The Automatic Hurt Maker consists of the same 24-inch metal ruler, but the modification is Angry Dave not telling you he is testing it. Evidently, the element of surprise is vital to his research.

Chapter I

I might have to get rid of my dog Crappy. As you know, Crappy has been my pet for 97 years now. I found Crappy one day eating the leather seats out of my custom mechanized battle armor suit, so I took him in as my own son. Crappy didn't like being my son, so I took him in again as my pet dog.

As you know, Crappy has a funny little quirk. He has to “make a boom-boom” at the same time each day. That time is basically between the hours of morning through nighttime. Now all this boom-boom is great for compost, but I found out the hard way that compost in not good for carpets.

I tried putting him out during the day, but Crappy, having had a human brain implanted around his existing dog brain, had the combined intellect of a really smart dog-man. So every time I tried to put him out, he would hot-wire my anti-giant killer robot assault hovercraft, and go on a shopping spree at the Big & Tall Men's store. I've got enough Heavy Duty non-stick underpants to last a lifetime.

Chapter 1

My relentless search for the ultimate double bacon cheeseburger has finally gotten out of hand. The other day while Kiel the Destroyer and I were out looking for lunch--or what Kiel the Devastator calls "looking for lunch"--we came across a sign on which was written, "Try our Ultimate Double Bacon Cheeseburger now Improved!" I thought, "If this was truly an ultimate double bacon cheeseburger, how could they make improvements to it?"

Kiel, completely aware of this glaring oxymoron, had reached for an invention my very good friend, Angry Dave, had made for him. As you recall, that's what Angry Dave does, invents things. This invention was called the "Wrongolizer." This Wrongolizer could make someone admit that he or she was, in fact, wrong about something. It looked just like a large hand gun, but this one actually fired real bullets, unlike most large hand guns.

Kiel approached the pimply youth behind the counter to inquire about the sign. I recognized the youth from an article I had read called, "Let's All Tease the Tragic Pimple Boy." In this article it explained how working at this fast food place--not to mention a lifetime of bad hygiene, poor breeding, and greasy food--had rendered his face tragically teased. As a result of this pimple-ing and teasing, the youth had built himself a fully functioning, life-sized and anatomically correct replica of Naked-Tron, the robotic crime fighting gay porn star, complete with stirrups.

It just so happened that this replica of Naked-Tron, the robotic crime fighting gay porn star, complete with stirrups, had gotten a job at that very same fast food place and was currently working the grill (and working it well.) Hearing the commotion at the counter, Naked-Tron sprang from his knees to assist the Tragic Pimple Boy.

When Kiel saw the anatomically correct nude robot, he screamed like a little school boy who was just seconds away from being thrashed by the robotic crime fighting gay porn star's Appendage of Justice. Yeah, we both laugh about it now.

Chapter 1

Professor Mojo teaches a course on World Domination and Villainy at the local community college. He also teaches Spanish and Home Ec. The Professor's lifelong dream (not unlike my own) is to build a series of orbiting death-ray platforms high above the planet and rule the world with an iron fist, forcing the human race to harvest urine from the rare and dangerous Urine Monkey.

One day, on my way to class, I was attacked by a horde of evil drone attack modules, loosed on mankind by the evil and mad Dr. Geoff (Roger). I quickly activated my non-sticking, evil drone defensive three-ring binder with built-in calculator and espresso maker, which had just been in the shop because it kept pinching my finger when I closed it. The battle was brief, but my three-ring binder was victorious.

After the battle, but still on my way to class, My three-ring binder and I noticed that the cybernetic implant in my brain was informing me, "Today is Wednesday." The best thirty bucks I ever spent.

The subject of Prof. Mojo's class today was villainous ways to dominate the world using orbiting death-ray platforms and monkey urine. He always has the best topics. I reached into my genetically-enhanced hollow point backpack and retrieved my computerized, non-stick, urine-resistant pen to take notes. But, alas, during the battle, one of the evil drone attack modules had broken the container of monkey urine I happen to be bringing to class for extra credit. The spill had depleted the non-stick, urine-resistant coating, and the pen's computer chip was destroyed. I really liked that pen; it was <u>really</u> the best thirty bucks I ever spent.

Chapter I

So my telepathic, evil-genius two-year-old twin, daughters, known only as "The Twins," are well on their way to fulfilling their lifelong dream (not unlike my own) of world domination. As you remember, The Twins communicate only through a combination of dirty diapers and breaking expensive things I think are nice. On a lighter note, they have come up with a really cute nickname for me; they call me "More-Juice-Daddy!"

It seems that The Twins have plans, as best as I can figure, to destroy the world starting with my cat biles-of-the-world limited edition collectors set, a set which cost me tens of dollars, including shipping.

They began the day with a rousing game of "topple the furniture" followed by "hide the tuna sandwich in the VCR." Then it was time for The Twins to continue working on their command center and battle fortress. The fortress is being constructed using state of the art "couch cushion technology."

The Twins' weapon of choice is a platoon of tiny evil non-stick robotic ponies. The ponies only attack while you are napping on the couch. They go for the eyes first and then the groin. Another weapon in The Twins's arsenal is the Nerf ™ Ball-O-Doom. This harmless looking ball, when thrown, hones in on the most breakable thing in the room and sends it crashing to the ground.

The other day, The Twins and I went to the local Burger-Monster™ for an ultimate double bacon cheeseburger and a and a Box-o'-Fun Super Wonderful Meal™ for the girls. Now the ultimate double bacon cheeseburger was, shall I say, less than "ultimate" and the Box-o'-Fun Super Wonderful Meal™ consisted of a hamburger, something in a small translucent paper pouch that smelled just a little like French fries, a two ounce cup of Sugar Coma Cola™, and a wonderful little toy. The toy was based on the latest kids movie, "Daddy, Buy Me That Now!" The toy was the loveable character, "Chokie, the Bite-Sized Piece of Jagged Plastic." Next week's toy is going to be "Jabby, the Really Sharp Stick." I can hardly wait until they have "Burney, the Loveable Pack of Matches" and his pet, "Wadded-Up Ball of Oily Rags."

Chapter 1

I think my cybernetic brain implant with integrated web browser and espresso maker might not be working right. Oops, can't talk now.

More on that later.

Chapter 1

It is common in Native American cultures for an individual to have a spirit guide. Some are bears, wolves and even raccoons. My spirit guide is a rust stain on the tile around my bathtub. I find myself entranced at its simple wisdom, beauty, and slow-witted logic.

This spirit guide helps me solve troubling personal questions like, "Why am I here?" "What is the meaning of life?" and "Who's your friend Mr. Chubby-wubby?"

My spirit guide informs me that I am, in fact, Mr. Chubby-wubby's friend. On closer examination, I have found that the spirit guide is actually a surveillance device placed in every home built after 1929. The advice given to me is actually read by the monitoring agent from a government-issued manual: What If the Subject Thinks You Are His Spirit Guide?

Armed with this new information, I now enjoy misleading whoever is on the other side of the device. I will pretend to fall asleep and start drowning in the tub water. That freaks them out every time.

Chapter I

You try to do the right thing. I went to my monthly tax audit and public pants-down spanking the other day. This month there was some kind of discrepancy about my taxes. I tried writing-off the mileage on my Stealth enhanced Bionic Jet-pack that I use for my white slave/drug smuggling business I run out of the phone booth down the street. Well, the auditor, Mr. Richard Head, got all "freaked-out" about something...

Now, it seems, that you can't claim the money you spend to get some of your ho's teeth fixed as a business expense either. When did these tax laws get changed?

Chapter 1

The brutal onslaught of the super-intelligent genetically-enhanced dog-men has slowed down a bit. That's good, because the defending forces of the Supreme Commander are in desperate need of SprayCO™ spray-on bullet repellant.

I was on my way to the corner post office for some stamps and my weekly mind sweep/public rectal examination, when the local police stopped me for a routine officer boredom violation. The fine was a public pants down spankin' and thirty bucks each. And I went on about my business.

Further down the road I saw my very good friend, Chief Drinking Bare. As I told you in my last letter, the chief lost his teeth and desire to bathe when his fireworks stand/cigar lounge caught fire back in '91. The good thing is that he rebuilt his entire business. Now he uses a paper bag instead of a fireworks stand, and he doesn't sell fireworks or cigars; he just drinks and urinates on my door. I am very proud of him.

The chief was having a heated discussion with his very good friend Moe Foe. I think Moe Foe is either very small or invisible. I know he is real because, although I have never seen him, I have smelled him. Chief ended his discussion with Moe as I got close to him; it was probably a private conversation. Now, the Chief is a skilled magician even if he has just the one trick. It goes something like this: the Chief says, “Hey man, give me a dollar!” Then he takes the money and wonders off. Hours later I will find him in a very deep sleep in a pool of someone's vomit. When I ask him for my dollar back he acts like he has never met me before. That one just kills me.

Chapter 1

My very good friend Angry Dave told me once, "There is no problem so big that they haven't made an even bigger gun to solve it." The thing I like most about Angry Dave is that he's pro-active. He is currently working on his newest invention. As you recall, that's what Angry Dave does, invents things. This new invention is called the "Advantage-olizer." It is loosely based on the old west "Equalizer," which was a revolving six-shooter. Angry Dave thought, "What is the point of being equal in that kind of situation?" Angry Dave thought if one six-shooter made things equal then more six-shooters would be an advantage. The new invention is basically three six-shooters taped together.

Many of Angry Dave's inventions involve taping things together. One time, in a response to the "build a better mouse trap" issue, Angry Dave taped two cats to an angry and frightened Doberman. The thinking was that a cat is just about the best mouse trap around so two of them taped together should be better. And the Doberman? Well, let's just say that the Doberman was motivation for the cats to stay focused on the job at hand.

Dave wishes that he was the inventor of tape. "I wish I would have invented tape," he says. Dave tried to tape some tape together one time but tape, being transparent perfection dispensed from a roll, was only rendered useless by the addition of more tape. "Paste is also a good invention, but it has one disadvantage: it is not tape," said Dave. Paste is a very misleading adhesive. You're not supposed to eat paste, and yet it's non-toxic and minty-fresh-tasting. The jar of paste comes with a little "spoon," which is not really a spoon at all. It's a "paste applicator" that just happens to look and act just like a spoon for non-toxic, minty-fresh-tasting, delicious paste.

Now we have all heard the popular childhood nursery rhyme, "Revenge of Paste Man": a story about a kid who use to eat paste and was then poisoned by a trusted teacher, but instead of being killed, was turned into Paste Man, the minty-fresh non-toxic crime fighting superhero made out of paste. But before he was a superhero, Paste Man went crazy and almost killed the teacher and kicked the crap out of half a dozen cops. I think the message is clear: shut up and eat your paste.

Chapter 1

There was another explosion at the BurgerTech Research Center today. As you remember, Burger-Tec is devoted to developing "the Ultimate Double Bacon Cheeseburger." The institute was established in memory of my very good friend, Kiel the Destroyer. Not because he died or anything like that, but because of the tragic "Naked-Tron, life-size, fully functioning and anatomically correct robotic crime fighting gay porn star and his Appendage of Justice" incident. No one liked seeing that.

I heard a rumor once that they had, in-fact, developed the technology to build a truly "Ultimate" Double Bacon Cheeseburger. Professor Mojo, head researcher at the National Institute of Baconology and Spray-on Monkey Urine, had discovered some disturbing data. It seems that it would require 30 Bazillion tera-kamz of energy to cook all the bacon required to complete the burger. Professor Mojo explained, "The only way of generating that amount of energy is with a controlled 'putting an angry cat in a tub of water' reaction, and we're not able to do that safely. . . Yet!" Another theory was to use the grease from the already cooked bacon to fuel the cooking process. But noted physicist and campfire expert Dr. Pete McMeat explained, "The laws of thermodynamics and entropy would not allow for a productive, sustained reaction of that sort, and the black smoke makes the food taste bad."

My biggest fear is that the scientists and genetically-enhanced race of super-human fast food workers at the BurgerTech Research Center have actually been attempting to control these terrifying forces of nature. If we build the "Ultimate" Double Bacon Cheeseburger, won't someone else try to build an even more "Ultimate" Double Bacon Cheeseburger, and so on, until one day, an evil super intelligent monster computer builds the most "Ultimate" Double Bacon Cheeseburger of them all. There would be no stopping it.

Chapter I
All Swell That End Swell

The devil spawn child, Kevin, knocked over my trash cans again. When last we saw our hero, he had just moved to a community called Simpleton. Now this town of Simpleton is what I like to call "a nice place to be from." I was introduced to my new neighbors in the form of a police raid on my house. It seems that the neighbors mistook my minding my own business for a white slavery and gun smuggling ring being run out of my house, and called the police. It's a common mistake.

I think the neighbors are called the Damnitnow's, because the mom will call Kevin by his full name: "Kevin Damnitnow!"

Now, Kevin is a very gifted child. He is almost eight years old, and it looks like he will be potty trained some time this year. It sure will be good to see him move on to pull-ups. Kevin is also very smart: he can count all the way up to two. His mother works with him on his counting out in the yard. She will say, "Kevin Damnitnow, One! Two!" but she never gets to three. Sometimes she will start over and over like, "Kevin Damnitnow, One! Two! One! Kevin Damnitnow! One! Two! One! Two! Kevin Damnitnow!" It's great to see parents taking an active roll in the child's education.

Kevin's lifelong dream (not unlike my own) is to some

day be a real-life genetically-enhanced bionic attack dog-man with kung-fu action, and fight for the forces of the Overlord in the Urine-Wars. His mother, a virtual planet of a woman, is helping him fulfill his dream by putting his helmet and retractable dog leash on him when they go out in public.

Chapter 1
The Buoy Who Would Beacon

By most accounts, it is not a good idea to list "Can dance like a freek-o-zoid" as an "Additional Skill" on your resume, especially if your dancing is below freek-o-zoid standards. Nonetheless, my promotion at LingoTec finally came through. I got promoted to the LingoTec Experimental Research Center, LERC for short. As you recall, LingoTec is the third largest developer of technical sounding words and business acronyms.

The research project I am working on right now is something called the "Rhetorical Answer." It's an answer to a question, which doesn't need to be asked. The best examples of a rhetorical answer would be "Dog did it" and "I don't want a spanking."

I can't wait until I have a chance to use some of the experimental equipment at the lab like the 30-mile-wide pronoun accelerator. We introduce a pronoun into a specially constructed paragraph. Then, by removing all common and proper nouns, we accelerate this pronoun to incredible speeds. Once the pronoun has reached a certain speed, we use a preposition at the end of a sentence to smash it with. Then we study the fragments. We have discovered that pronouns are made up of even smaller particles or "letters." We have named these "letter things," for lack of a better term, "Senior Fuentes"

Senior Fuentes"

The downside to this whole thing is the head researchers have been really pushing me to show them a few dance steps. I guess you really have to be careful what you put on your resume; they might check.

Chapter I
How to be a Rock Star

I tell everyone the same thing: the first step to being a rock star is to tell everybody you meet, "I'm a rock star." This is very important, because if you don't tell them, how will they know?

Step Two: During conversations, make many references about yourself in the third person as if you were on the other side of the room and just made eye contact with yourself.

Step C: Every time you stay at a motel, hotel, or even a friend's house, be sure to trash the room. If you don't trash the room, at least take a towel and tell people you trashed the room. If you stay at a friend's house, try to get their wallet or handgun.

Step 4: When eating at a restaurant, always send the food back, because it has "bad energy." Most of the time, the cooks will spit in the food and send it back to the table. The next time, refuse to accept the food, because you wanted the chicken. Keep this going as long as possible alternating between the chicken and poor napkin placement.

Step One: Have lots of stories about how you and "Mick" use to hang out. When they ask if you know Mick Jagger (and they will), tell them "Not Mick Jagger, the other Mick."

Step To: Keep a box of plastic forks and lots of napkins in your coat pocket. Rock stars know you can never, and I mean never, have too many napkins. And what happens if someone gives you some free pie, but you don't have a fork? That would just be sad.

Step Last: Every good rock star knows this one. After telling them that you are a rock star, ask every stranger you see on the street, “What city is this?” Then ask them, “What day is this?” Next ask the stranger if “they hear that, too.” If the stranger is still there, ask them to smell your shirt, because you think it smells just a little like monkey semen.

Chapter I

Some days are just better than others. One such day happened to me just yesterday. I was on my way to work when I looked down. Much to my surprise, I saw that I had forgotten to put pants on. Most of the time forgetting to put pants on before you go out in public is not a good thing, but today was St. Spankin's Day: the national holiday celebrating Saint Paddlebottom MacSpankin. It is the custom on this day to not wear one article of clothing you would usually wear, preferably your pants. If you forget to not wear an article of clothes, you get a pants-down spankin'. On the other hand, if you remember to not wear your pants, it is the custom to get a pants-down spankin'.

"Lucky me," I said out loud. "St. Spankin's Day."

Being thrilled at this turn of events, I made the "chalk one up for me" motion in the air. At this moment a carload of youngsters was passing buy. This car was probably in need of repair because it kept making a loud boom-d-doom sound and was about six inches too close to the ground. I so very much wanted to make a funny comment about this car, but I could only come up with, "Hey, mister, your car's broken." The car stopped and most of the youngsters got out and started punching and kicking me for the less-than-humorous statement and not having any pants on. I tried to explain that it was the custom to give a full body and head beating on Massive Blunt Trauma Day and not St.Spankin's Day. Oh, did I tell you, this is one of the "other days" I was talking about.

Chapter 1

Pat McGroin was raced to the emergency room, the terrible "open-faced sandwich accident" still fresh in his mind and hair. I remember the ambulance driver saying that this was the worst case of peanut butter exposure he had ever seen.

Pat's on-line service offers women the use of an eligible bachelor for a fee. The fee is thirty bucks. And the service is the guy drinking beer and watching sports on TV.

This thirty bucks is to cover the cost of beer and the pay-per-view nude female wrestling match. For some reason, Pat McGroin thought that women want to give men money so the guy could drink beer and watch professional naked women's sports.

Chapter 1

Dr. Nude, also known as "the Fabulous Dr. Nude," also known as Senior Fuentes, or Dr. Peter Hangnout, had been bombarding the city with his robotic attack chickens for weeks now. The attack chickens were launched from an orbiting death-ray platform high above the planet. He had been resorting to the chicken assault, because the death-ray had been switched to Boogie instead of Death, and then the knob fell off and rolled behind the dishwasher.

Dr. Nude's orbiting death-ray platform, quite by accident, was shaped like a mattress with a large urine stain, but if you looked hard enough, the stain on the orbiting death-ray platform looked a lot like Jesus. It wasn't so bad at first, having robotic attack chickens launched from a likeness of Jesus. On day four of the assault, I ventured outside to watch as the orbiting image of our Lord and Savior darkened the sky with robotic attack poultry. Much to my surprise, the streets were filled with religious pilgrims here to worship the orbiting death-ray platform and choke the city's transit infrastructure and clog public restrooms.

Being completely outraged at this public display of religious nudity... That's right; I forgot to mention the pilgrims believed that the orbiting Christ-shaped assault stain wanted his followers to be naked in front of my house.

As I was saying, being completely outraged at this public display of religious nudity, I began launching the Pronoun torpedoes. As you remember, the Pronoun torpedoes were developed by the LingoTec defense division. The big selling point is that the targeting system is very "warmonger-friendly." You just program "shoot it" or "kill them" or "blow that up" and off it goes.

The first barrage of Pronoun torpedoes went off without a hitch. This time, being careful to put the hitch on, the second barrage went off with a hitch. With a bright flash of light, Dr. Nude's orbiting death-ray platform began its long fall to earth. "That oughta learn him," I said to myself, and anyone else who could hear me. The now-angry nude religious pilgrims began to disperse, because their orbiting urine stain savior no longer ruled the skies.

Just as I thought that the entire ordeal was over, the burning death-ray platform crashed into the corporate headquarters of BaconWorld, the international chain of bacon-related theme parks, also known as "the Devil's Lunch Box!" The now-confused religious fanatics took this as a sign that the orbiting urine stain had defeated the devil or at least his lunch box and it was time to celebrate by parking on my lawn.

Chapter l

The angry giant cougars came back to our neighborhood again. I was taking my medical waste to the recycling bin when I was confronted by the neighbor dog, Humpy, who also goes by the name Senior Fuentes. As you remember, Humpy is desperately trying to convince me that my leg is far too sexy for its own good. Unfortunately, my leg had taken a vow of celibacy shortly after Humpy moved in.

Chapter I

And Tim knows exactly how to fix it. That is what I tell everyone. You see, Tim is an insane evil genius. He refers to himself as "Tim, fixer of broken things, repairer of the unrepaired, maker of working things which once worked but then didn't work until I fixed them just a minute ago." But Tim has little or nothing to do with this...

Most of my life I have felt that I was a lesbian trapped in a heterosexual man's body. I heard one time about a lesbian trapped in an elevator with a priest, a rabbi, and a sheep, but that story didn't apply to me that much. I have been in an elevator with a rabbi, but never trapped in one or with a sheep or a priest, and I've seen a priest trapped by a roving pack of priest-hunting lesbians, and they might have been Jewish. I also heard once about a blond, brunette, and a redhead trapped in a lifeboat with a magic lamp and three wishes. Who knows? They could have been lesbians. But that's neither here nor there.

My very good friend Art Carter's neighbor, Wanda B. Amann, just happens to be the chief of a friendly tribe of non-priest hunting lesbians, and I think she's a brunette judging from the hair under her armpits and the fact that she smells like peroxide much of the time.

One day, on my way home from Spankin' Town, I ran into Wanda and my very good friend Art Carter. I apologized and helped them back onto their feet. They just happened to be on their way to a lesbian demonstration down at City Hall and asked if I would like to go along. I asked them if it was a free event and would they need any volunteers from the audience. Wanda shook her head and asked Art if I was the one who lives over by the lead paint factory. Well, you know me. I am never one to turn down watching lesbians give a free demonstration, so off we went.

It turns out that I misunderstood what Wanda and Art meant about the "demonstration," but as luck would have it at the "rally," I happened to run into my very good friend Professor Mojo, who teaches a class on Lesbian Heckling down at the community college. He also teaches Applied Particle Physics and Spanish.

Anxious to earn some extra credit, I began assisting Professor Mojo in his heckling. All I can say is lesbians are a lot stronger than they look and when it comes to "Free Demonstrations," you get what you pay for.

Chapter 1

I discovered that my arms are about 26 feet too short. I think the ideal situation would be if I had 28-foot long telescoping arms with the ability to retract them, so they wouldn't scare the children or lesbians. My very good friend Art Carter thinks I might be off my nut for wanting to have 28-foot retractable or possibly telescoping arms instead of the standard issue human arms. He would tell me, "You have gotta be off your nut, Senior Fuentes." That's kind of how he is.

Who wouldn't want to have nearly 30-foot long arms and not have to advertise to the world, "Hey, look at me; I have really long arms! Why don't you ask me to reach something really high up for you?" I think that would get old in a hurry. They would have to be retractable, because most people don't want their kids or lesbians to see that kind of thing, and for goodness sake, think of the lesbians!

Another suggestion Art Carter gave me was, instead of retractable or telescoping arms, what about elastic or some kind of space-age rubber-like composite arms, which could snap back into place after being extended. I informed Art Carter that the recoil action of elastic arms "snapping" back into place could cause serious damage to me and surely any children or lesbians standing near me. He obviously is not thinking about the lesbians.

This all started when the neighbor kid, Kevin Damnitnow, scared my pet kite into the tree. It was about 28 feet up this tree. The base of the tree must have been three feet thick and, as we all know, I am terrified of thickness. So I set off in search of a long-reaching or poking device with some kind of hook or adhesive on the end. I would like it to be about 26 feet long with a sort of handle or gripping attachment for ease of use. And you can't go wrong if it's non-sticking.

After hours of searching in vain, I decided to go with the retractable or telescoping arms. People think you're a few bricks shy of a dollar when you ask for a non-sticking, 26 to 28 foot long poking or reaching device with some sort of hook or adhesive on the poking/reaching end and a handle or gripping attachment for ease of use. As is often the case, my very good friend Art Carter gave me these words of wisdom: "When life throws you a curve ball, don't try to drown your sorrows in a fool's dream of retractable or telescoping arms. The somewhat attainable goal of finding a non-stinking, poking or reaching device with a hook or adhesive at the poking end and an easy grip handle attachment will just distract you from what you are truly searching for. Instead, overcome your fear of thickness and climb the tree. That, or find a trained monkey." Sometimes I think Art might be loosing it.

Next week: Revenge of The Throbulator!!!

Chapter I
The Throbulator

The latest improvements to the Throbulator have only been documented as "now with 33% added improvement." What this really means, I don't know. I only know that using the Throbulator in conjunction with the Spankotron can cause severe throbulation and possibly an acute case of spankosis. On my way home from the hospital I met my very good friend Art Carter at the corner of Third and Third.

Art was on his way to see the stump doctor. Art had just lost his hand in a horrible paste tasting accident which left him left-handed-less. Now Art is a very reasonable person and is not upset about the left-handed-less-ness. He feels that everything balances out in the end. Art speculates that somewhere down the road, he might be infected with some exotic virus which mutates the infected to grow two left hands or find himself in some kind of medical experiment gone horribly wrong and loses his right hand as well. Possibly, he had multiple left hands in a past life and owes one or two in return, kind of like karma. So you see how everything balances out in the end.

It seems that Art Carter's stump was giving off a bad or "funky" smell. The doctor diagnosed Art with stumpfunktosis and prescribed a regiment of stump defunktification.

The stump defunktification process begins with the effected or infected funky stump preparation by submersion in a tub of defunktifying paste. At first, Art was hesitant, in part from his new found phobia of paste but mostly he just didn't like the smell of the paste. “The paste smells a little bit like waffles,” he would tell me. As you remember, my very good friend Art Carter could eat his own body weight in waffles as long as they were slathered in minty-fresh paste, ergo, the problem inherent.

Once the paste is removed from the funky stump, an ointment is applied. Quite by coincidence, this ointment tastes, not unlike me, just a bit like chicken. Art likes things that taste just a bit like chicken but hates things that taste exactly like chicken. I think Art likes things that taste just a bit like chicken because they taste less like chicken than chicken does. But that is neither here nor there.

Finally, Art puts a lifelike hand thing on the end of his stump for reasons that are two-fold. First, the lifelike hand thing has some kind of deodorizer in it to control the “funkyness,” and second, to make Art look less like a freak of nature. It just goes to show you, Art imitates life. Or, at least a lifelike hand thing.

Chapter I
Dr. Suess on the "Juice"

Have I told you the story of Doug Kaboom. Doug Kaboom kept a messy, messy room.

He never went outside; Doug stayed in his room. He never picked up a wash cloth, a dust rag, or broom, Doug was so messy, alone in his room.

When dinner was ready, would Doug sit at the table? He would eat in his room and watch porn on cable.

"When you are done eating, pick up your dishes!" "Okay," says Doug, as his wife nags and bitches. The dishes don't get washed. Doug pitches his dishes under the mattress and ignores his wife's wishes.

The dishes piled up in unwashed stacks. The food was caked on; the plates all had cracks. All of it stacked up by empty six-packs.

The clutter consisted of dishes no less, but so much more went into this mess.

Piles of socks, potato chip bags, newspapers, underpants, and urine soaked rags. Paint thinner, gas can, and old porno mags.

His mess got so big it started to pile up. Up in the sky, the mess in a pile was stacked up so high, about a mile up. Such a big mess so stacked up could make almost anyone sick or throw-up. Then one day, Doug's wife came aknocking. By the look on her face, Doug was in for a talking. "Look at this mess!" Doug felt attacked. "I've had it with you; now get your shit packed!" He packed up his clothes and his pornography quick. He packed his TV; he packed all of his shit.

"You'll take me back," Doug slyly snooted. Doug's wife calmly pulled out a shotgun and shooted. Because Doug was messy and stuck in a rut, his wife flipped out and put buckshot in his butt. And to this day Doug says she is the nut.

Chapter 1
Revenge of Paste Man: a Love Story

The sign over head, in bold letters read,
"Don't eat the paste," that's what it said.
Marvin MacMeater was a big paste eater,
But not a very good bold letter reader.
The teacher would say, "Don't eat the paste."
But Marvin didn't listen; the paste he would taste.
He loved very much the taste of the paste.
He could eat twenty or thirty jars in one place.
The teacher would say, "Marvin Mac Meater,
Stop eating that paste. No one likes a paste eater."
Then one day, the teacher tried a trick.
He put something in the paste to make Marvin sick.
He put something in and sealed up the jars,
Knowing full well he could get life behind bars.
"Try to eat that, we'll see if you can.
Nobody could eat that paste, except maybe Paste Man."
But Marvin kept eating, taste after taste,
Tasting and eating the poisonous paste.
Suddenly he stopped and dropped the paste can.
He started to turn into some kind of evil Paste Man.

Now being Evil Paste Man wasn't so bad.
But something had made Evil Paste Man go mad.
It was the sign over head, “Don't eat the paste.”
Evil Paste Man began to give every one a “taste.”
“Ha Ha,” he laughed. “Now you eat my paste.”
He pasted and pasted everyone he faced.
He tried for the teacher, to give him a taste.
But the teacher was quicker, so Paste man got maced.
He put the can in his face and he maced and he maced.
“Ha Ha,” said the teacher. “How do you like that taste?”
When Marvin MacMeater hit the floor with a yelp,
The other kids cried and screamed out for help.
The teacher stared down at his empty mace can.
He stared and he stared at the evil paste man.
He was staring at Marvin askew on the floor
When came quite a clatter and in-kicked the door.
The cops hollered, “Freeze,” and one pulled out a stick,
A shiny black stick, and he swung it 'round quick.
The stick found its mark on the teacher's left knee.
He clutched! He tumbled! Involuntarily peed!
Another blow fell in the small of his back,
Then one on his arm! His leg! Whack whack whack!
The teacher cried out with every hot stinging,
And the cops were distracted with their Rodney Kinging.
They couldn't have noticed Marvin MacMeater
Scooping fingers of paste to his hungry paste-eater.
The paste-charged MacMeater was starting to glow
Like a three-thousand-gigawatt paste dynamo!
He stood and observed the abusive display.
He thought and concluded in his new pasty way.
He pasted up one cop, then pasted up two.
He pasted them all up, and when he was through
There were cops on the floor and cops on the wall.
There were cops pasted to the lights in the hall.
The teacher looked up through eyes that were swollen;

He was bleeding a lot from a blow to his colon.
He asked the Paste Man, he asked Marvin MacMeater,
Why he had stopped the militant beaters.
But Marvin wasn't talking; he just turned away.
Marvin was above the foolish human ways.
He went out of the classroom. He walked pastily by.
He pastily look up into the pasty blue sky.
Then Marvin MacMeater, who couldn't read writing
Reaped the rewards of his years of paste-biting.
Into the world, into the cosmos he went.
And with his passing came a discernable scent.
Everything now had a light pasty tint,
And everything now smelled a bit...
Just a bit like mint.

Chapter I

My very good friend Art Carter has been channeling the long dead spirit of Nostradamus. He recently told me one of his predictions. I have to admit that he might have lost his touch.

It went like this:

"In the third week of a month with the letter 'M' or 'E' somewhere in its name, the great leader of a nude tribe of people made entirely out of cake, or maybe bread, will open a package addressed to Senior Fuentes. At least it looks like a package from where I am sitting. The package will contain some kind of object. The object will look cheap, but actually some one paid way too much for it. The object is made of a material that looks like wood but is not wood at all. The person that gave the package to the other person is from somewhere originally but moved a couple times until he or she finally stopped moving around and just settled down.

"The leader of the nude tribe will thank the other guy for the gift and then secretly look for the receipt so he can exchange it for something else, probably some pants or a nice jacket suit, unless the item was not worth very much. I don't think it was very expensive so he probably couldn't get a suit, because suits sometimes cost like $1000 or something for a nice wool one."

Chapter I

A new and dangerous virus has been detected. If you receive an e-mail with the subject line "Dangerous Virus Enclosed!!! Please open me suckers!!!" don't open it.

When asked about the new malicious virus, a spokeswoman from IBM was quoted as saying, "If you don't stop calling me at home I will have you arrested." This is obviously in an effort to cover up the virus and the conspiracy to cover up the cover up conspiracy and other associated plots. When asked about the cover up and the associated conspiracy plots, the spokesman from BurgerMonster™, Senior Fuentes was quoted as saying, "What the hell are you talking about? Get out of my restaurant!" Rich Richmanson--the step-son of Manfred Manfieldson, noted mumbling street person and authority on tin foil hats and poor dental hygiene-- when asked about the virus and associated conspiracy and cover-up plots,

(mumbled)"...Stain.... monkey urine... cu.!@&*! Where did I put that... !@#*&? BITCH!" And then put on his tin foil hat.

An authority on conspiracies noted, "It is a well-known fact that if someone does not want you to know about a conspiracy they will try to cover it up or deny that there is a conspiracy at all. Just like all those people wearing tin foil hats to block the mind control beam. That's just what the alien overlords want you to think. It has to be lead, lead, I tell you! Tin just acts like an antenna!"

In an effort to try to stop this threat, we recommend that

you try not to be stupid if you can help it and only give out your credit card and social security numbers to phone solicitors who really, really sound like they are honest. Keep your TV viewing down to 6.3 minutes per day, because the government can see into your house and watch you while the TV is on. Never call and request a song on the radio, because that's how they find your brain frequency to beam the mind control ray. And finally, only listen to the voice in your head that tells you <u>not</u> to burn things. This is the only voice not controlled by the evil alien overlords bent on eating your internal organs and then harvesting their own flatulence to power the even <u>more</u> evil alien super-overlord's interstellar space ships. We have to act now!

Chapter I
The Unbearable Lightness of Bean

My very good friend Hamstring Schmeltermelter Von Pouch, who lives just down the street from the BurgerMonster™ restaurant, just ate his own body weight in salad. The sad end to that story is that his lifelong dream (not unlike my own) was to eat his own body weight in salad. Now, I am not saying that my lifelong dream was to eat my own body weight in salad; much the contrary. My lifelong dream was to have Hamstring eat my body weight in salad followed by a sensible after-dinner mint shaped like a 1957 Thunderbird. I personally think that salad is the green stuff you scrape into the trash after you are done eating your real food.

Having fulfilled his lifelong dream of eating his own body weight in salad, Hamstring fell into a very deep depression. The depression was caused when an orbiting death-ray platform shaped like a urine stained mattress fell from the sky and impacted with the earth directly on the site of the BaconWorld corporate headquarters. The depression must have been 300 feet wide and 100 feet deep. Hamstring should have seen it but was too sad that he had prematurely achieved his lifelong dream and felt he had nothing left to live for. I tried to help Hamstring out of this deep depression, but as you know, I am terrified of depths.

Falling deep into this depression, Hamstring finally hit rock bottom with a resounding “Ker-whack!” Stunned onlookers stared in awe as Hamstring bounced back up nearly 33% of the distance he had fallen. Hamstring, having little to no grasp of percentages or fractions, got a crash course in the mathematics of slamming into the rocky ground below. With this new-found knowledge of math, Hamstring began to understand the formula of what had just happened. He deduced that one cranium divided by one huge bolder equals 20% of his former mental capacity. But there is a positive side to this story. Hamstring has come up with a new lifelong dream (not unlike my own). It has something to do with using the brain thing or using language again or something like that. It's hard to tell.

Chapter 1

Farnsworth, the contagious biter monkey, had a grossly enlarged prostate. This condition was due in part to a discipline problem and the constant spanking the young monkey received.

As a young impressionable boy, I remember watching Captain Fromwell, the police lieutenant, spank his monkey Farnsworth for misbehaving. "Bad monkey!" he would say as he spanked. Cap'n Fromwell's lifelong dream (not unlike my own) was to command a mighty army of highly-trained ninja monkeys and rule the world with an iron fist. But alas, all of the ninja monkeys had high-paying union jobs at BurgerMonster™, so Cap'n Fromwell tried biter monkeys instead. Now, it is well known that biter monkeys are very receptive to <u>not</u> being trained and are highly training-resistant. They mostly excel at biting and this poses the beforementioned discipline problem.

One day while Farnsworth the biter monkey was at the store to pick up some beer and bite people, a pack of angry robotic infector rats infected Farnsworth with something to make him contagious and angry. Farnsworth was, for obvious reasons, upset with the whole "getting infected" thing and the "grossly enlarged prostate" situation, so he started a drunken crime spree. Well, I can tell you, Cap'n Fromwell was taken aback to hear of the drunken, contagious monkey crime spree so he put three bullets in Farnsworth's back. <u>One, two, three</u>.

Now this minor setback to Cap'n Fromwell is not stopping him from pursuing his dream of world domination. I'm just a little bit worried because Cap'n Fromwell is now thinking about using humper monkeys instead.

Chapter I
Alabaster Crumpp

Alabaster Crumpp liked a good pants down spankin'. He also liked pie with ice cream on top of it, Muslim-style: Allah mode. "I sure could go for a good pants down spankin' and then some pie with ice cream on it," he would say. Alabaster also liked to play the ponies and bet on the prostitute races. A recent addition to Alabaster's long list of vices was wagering on the Richard Richmanson, noted mumbling street person and authority on cheap wines and Random Odor Generator. He would insist that safe money was on it producing the smell of urine. But Alabaster liked the excitement of putting his money on "a kind of waffle smell."

One day, on my way home from BaconWorld®, I happened to spot Alabaster at the local Casa Del Pie Dojo Haas®. By the looks of it, Alabaster was on his fourth pie. "What-cha-doing, Alabaster?" I asked.

"Gettin' all pied-up for tonight," he said. Well, knowing that Alabaster had trouble holding his pie, I reminded him of his last pie binge. It resulted in him waking up in downtown Portland, ass all a blister, with a quarter jammed in his ear and the taste of Key lime and something else really bad still fresh in his mouth.

Later that same evening, I was out patrolling the streets in my genetically-enhanced, laser-guided, hollow-point llama-bot with retractable pencil sharpener, when I saw Alabaster piefully wandering toward Portland. But out of the corner of my one good eye I spotted Richard Ramjet Jr. coming closer. As you remember, Alabaster Crumpp's biggest fear (not unlike my own) is of Dick Ramjet, Jr. Just as I saw Dick Ramjet, Jr., I saw my very good friend Art Carter out of the corner of my other one good eye. It is a well-known fact that Richard Ramjet, Jr.'s greatest fear is of Art Carter, due in part to his freakishly huge penis--a penis so large it ran for Senator of Utah back in '84 but was defeated by a landslide.

Richard Ramjet, Jr. confronted Alabaster. Like something out of a poorly-written collection of short stories, Richard Ramjet, Jr. began demanding Alabaster's pie money. But, alas, Alabaster had spent all of his money earlier and was on his way to Portland to get some more. My very good friend Art Carter, knowing the terror his penis wrought, intervened. Richard Ramjet Jr., accepted the gruesome ultimatum and decided to take an I.O.U. for the strong-armed pie money. But the only pencil 'tween the three of them was too dull to scribe the note. In an attempt to avert a confrontation of epic and stomach-churning proportions, I quickly offered the use of my retractable pencil sharpener, because nobody really wanted to see that.

Chapter I
778.26 Foot-Pounds of Torque

It's like my dad use to tell me. He would say, "Son, shut the hell up or I'll knock the taste outta-yer mouth." He would also tell me, "Son, there is just one thing in this world you need to know: the amount of energy, measured in calories, of one BTU." He would never tell me how much that was. If I asked, he would tell me the "knock the taste outta-yer mouth" one again.

Now it is a well-known fact that one BTU represents 4,420.7057 calories of energy. It is also a well-known fact that I can't have anything nice. Case in point. One day I was enjoying some fries while having my uterus cleaned. I was explaining to the plumber the very fact that I can't have anything nice when I spilled tartar sauce on my Elvis-flavored suit jacket. Now tartar sauce never comes all the way out of clothes, thus proving my point. The uterus plumber, Harry Crack, explained that the only way to get tartar sauce out of anything Elvis is to rub liquor or BBQ pork ribs on it. I had been saving a very nice bottle of peach brandy for a special occasion but then decided that not only was this a special occasion but by using it to remove a tartar sauce stain, reinforced the fact that I can't have anything nice.

After applying most of the bottle to the stain, I remembered that the only thing that stains Elvis suits worse than tartar sauce is anything peach-flavored. With a chant of "What gets out peach flavor? What gets out peach flavor?" I rushed to the kitchen for my collection of pork fat. I was saving the pork fat for a special occasion, but that's neither here nor there.

I quickly rubbed the pork fat on the peach/tartar sauce stain. I then remembered that there was indeed something that stained Elvis suits worse than tartar sauce or peach flavor, and that would be pork fat. The plumber, Harry Crack, then spoke up. "The only way to get pork fat out is you gotta eat the fat."

That's right, eat the fat! I remembered that from a class Professor Mojo taught at the community college called: "Stain Removal and Other Good Excuses to Eat the Fat 101." I also remembered from the class: never ask a woman if she would like to "eat the fat," because it would result in a pan of scalding hot water being poured over your testicles.

I look back at the events of that day and think hindsight is 20/20, and if I knew then what I know now, I'd know now what I now know. And that is to say that peach brandy, pork fat, and, yes, tartar sauce are all flammable, and it is never a good idea to try to burn a stain out. I also don't recommend eating the fat or pouring scalding hot water over your testicles or for that matter having someone else do it for you. Life is basically long periods of mundanely enjoying your fries, interrupted by brief instances of fiery, pork-fueled epiphany, so exercise due caution.

Chapter I
Overwhelming Understatement

Diversity is the presence of multiple uniquenesses. This is not to say that it is the absence of a single sameness, but the presence of a single or multiple differences over a broad range of similar but uniquely different samenesses.

It is also the presence of identicalness being absent and the absence of identicalness being present.

Diversity is the culmination of some or many differences to form a unified oneness thus creating a single sameness. Ergo, an individual's differences, when added to a diverse group, gives every individual a similarity of being different. Although the differences are similar, these similarities are all quite different. It is this differentness that adds to our sameness within the diverse group.

Diversity means that we are all the same in that we are all uniquely similar in our differences. Each individual's differences are different thus adding to the overall diversity of the diversity. For example, "The more things change the more they stay the same," which is to say that constant change is constantly the same by continuing to change, unless it stops changing, which means that the constant change has changed to not changing any more.

This is a change in and of itself thus returning to the state of constant change, which means that it never really changed in the first place, meaning it stayed the same, which isn't change, now is it?

Staying the same, well, it just stays the same, I think.

Chapter I
Glad I'm Not Hugh

We all, for the most part, only get one shot at life. Only a very few lucky people get a second chance at life. I decided to pay for three chances at life up front but, as a consequence, couldn't afford the undercoating of Scotch-Guard™. So, as a result it's ended up looking like crap. My very good friend Art Carter opted to forgo his second chance at life altogether. He decided to get the freakishly huge penis instead. At first, this sounded like a good idea, but after the terrible "zipper-race" accident, he sort of regretted his choice. Nobody liked watching that.

The whole idea of a penis so huge it needs to register for the draft when it turns 18 generally intrigues most men. But I think I would rather have a big powerful ass instead, an ass powerful enough to haul very heavy things. Either that or a donkey or possibly a tractor… It's like my grandpa use to tell me. He would say, "Damn-it boy, that beer ain't gonna get it-self!" He would also tell me, "Damn-it boy, you think a huge John Thomas is gonna solve all your problems? Well it ain't! A huge penis never solved anything. You remember Ol' Senior Fuentes down at the grain silo; he had him a freakishly huge penis and children are still starvin' in China." Oh, how right he was.

Dr. P. Niss at the Research Center for Male Things says

that the size of a man's penis directly effects how attractive he thinks he is to the opposite sex. Unlike large breasts on the female, which actually does affect how attractive a woman is, the penis size ratio is only a false perceived attraction.

The size of your penis has nothing to do with the size of your feet or nose and is not an effective way to feed the starving children in China. Dr. P. Niss also explains that "A man's penis is directly related to a number of things, and that number is no more than 2." It seems that it's linked to a region in the brain called the delusional-thalamus cortex, a region of the brain that is responsible for making you think that you can "get a date with her" or "afford that Corvette."

The delusional-thalamus cortex is also stimulated by beer and televised contact sports. The penis is also linked to the wallet. A man will generally pull his wallet out if an opportunity to pull his penis out is present. Yes, the penis certainly comes with some baggage, and the idea that "size doesn't matter," well, let's just say that a man said that. So, I think that it's a good idea to save up your "chances at life" and use them not on a freakishly huge penis, but rather use your last chance at life to get the Corvette.

Next week: "The Pouch"

Chapter 1:
The good doctor's note book.

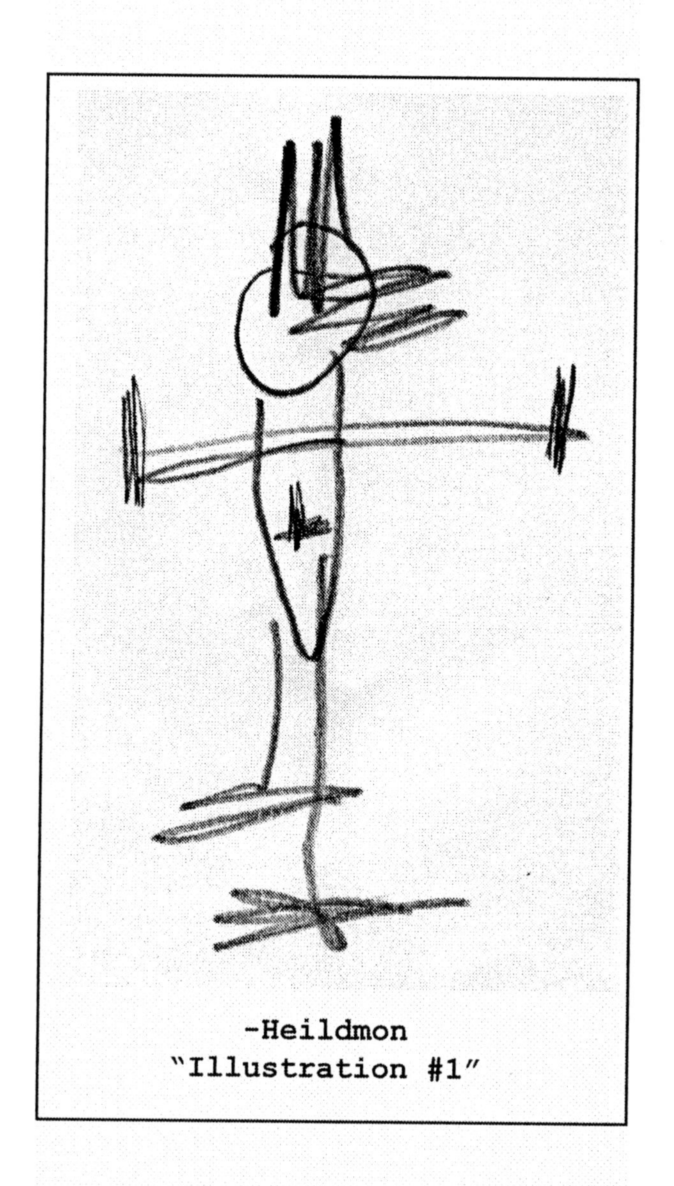

-Heildmon
"Illustration #1"

-Heildmon
"Illustration #1"

-Heildmon
"Illustration #1"

-Heildmon
"Illustration #1"

Dr. Heinrich Heildmon:
"fireshooters"

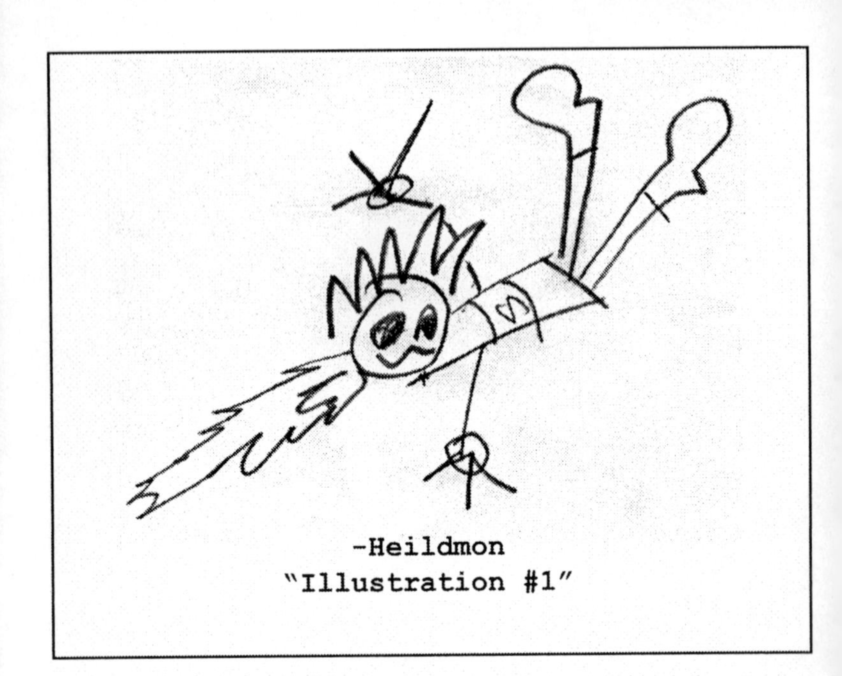

-Heildmon
"Illustration #1"

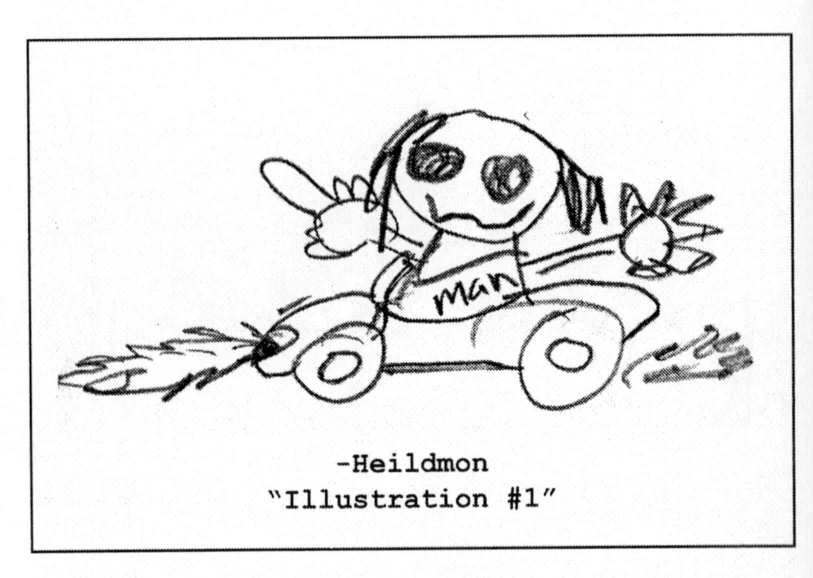

-Heildmon
"Illustration #1"

-Heildmon
"Illustration #1"

-Heildmon
"Illustration #1"

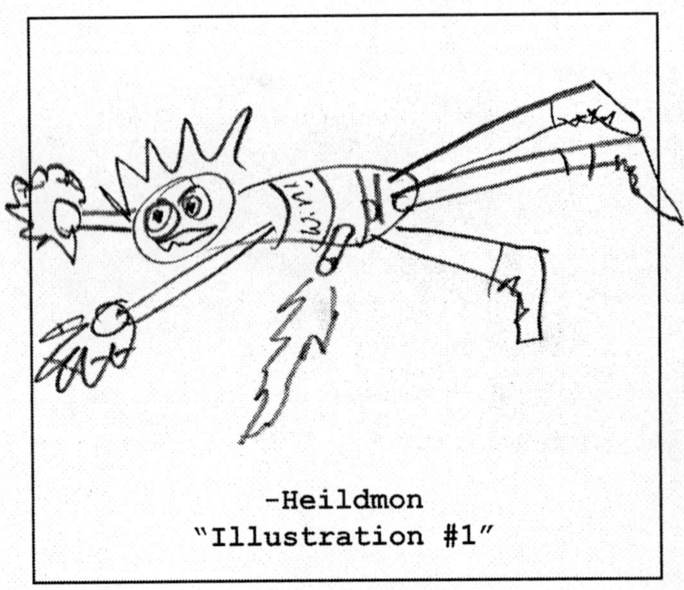

-Heildmon
"Illustration #1"

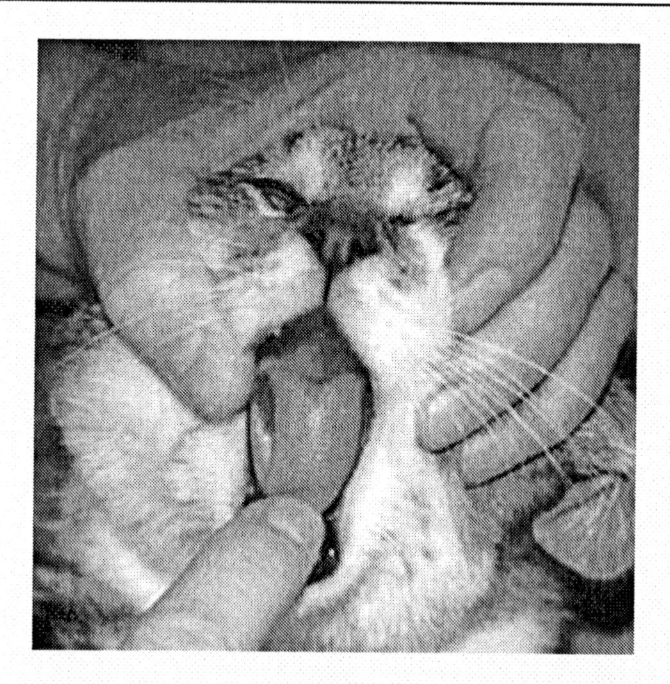

Mr. Scratches

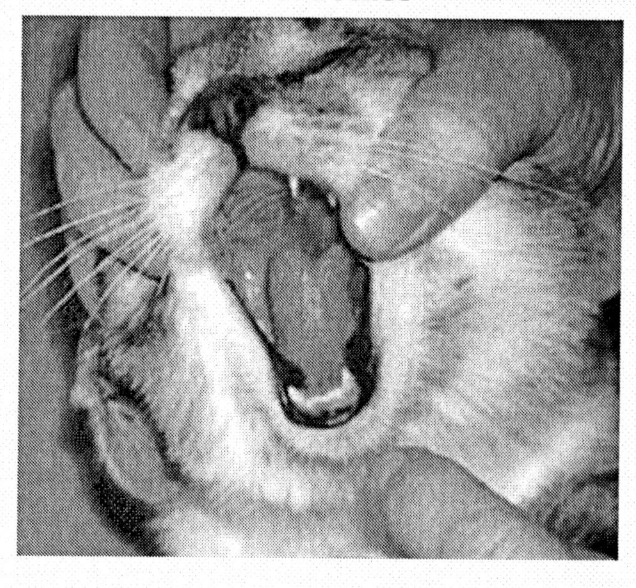

Senior Feuntes

Senior Feuntes with
young Heinrich Heildmon

The Evil Heildmon Twins
Gilgamesh and Agamemnon

-Hellamon
"Illustration #1"

-Heildmon
"Illustration #1"

-Heildmon
"Illustration #1"

-Heildmon
"Illustration #1"

-Heildmon
"Illustration #1"

-Heildmon
"Illustration #1"

-Heildmon
"Illustration #1"

-Heildmon
"Illustration #1"

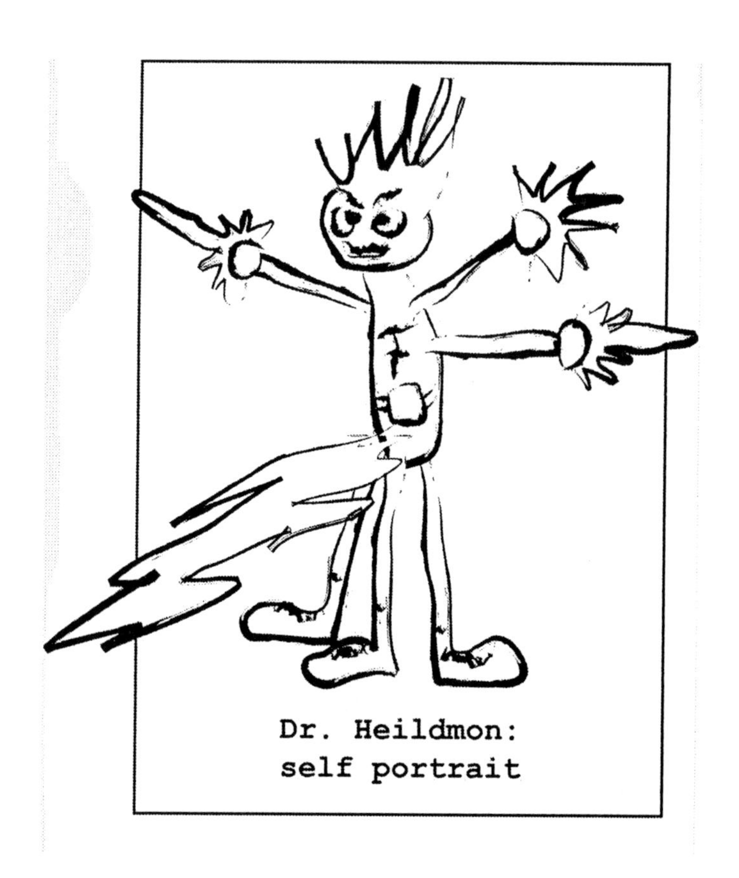

Dr. Heildmon:
self portrait

Chapter I
Mary Christmas and Her Magic Boogie Board

Many of us had make-believe or imaginary friends as a child. I had imaginary enemies who were constantly trying to "get me" or "beam radio signals into my brain to try to monitor and control my thoughts." A little game I would play was, in order to hide from the imaginary enemies, I would pretend that I was someone else. Having make-believe friends as a child is normal and many times adorable. However, having imaginary enemies and pretending to be other people to escape from the mind control beam is what psychologists and other mental health professionals call a paranoid schizophrenic. But that was just their way of trying to "get me."

One day on our way home from the WonderWaffle House of Pasta™, my very good friend Art Carter and I ran into Mary Christmas, the local crazy lady. As you remember, Mary Christmas is the local authority on make-believe enemies and radio signals being beamed into your brain. Being polite, Art Carter asked Mary how she was doing. We discovered that painfully there is an uncomfortable point in every conversation where you realize that you have nothing else to say. Unfortunately that point never arrives while Mary Christmas is talking to you.

Now, Mary has a very delicate mental condition, and Art, knowing this, approached the subject with due sensitivity: "Why don't you just shut the hell up, you freak of nature!" It's a well-known fact that the only truly selfless act of charity is one made while you are too drunk to remember it. And that the greatest gift that can be given is a pair of Russian-made night vision goggles. So armed with this knowledge and my pair of Russian-made night vision goggles, I quickly intervened by asking Mary how her other personalities were doing. She responded by removing from her shopping cart, which also doubled as her apartment and bathroom, a wooden plank with nails poking out of one end and the word "Boogie" scribed on it. She then mumbled something under her breath followed by the words, "And you're next, bitch!"

That was the day I lost control of my bowels and bladder. It was also the day I lost most of my left testicle, all of my colon, and most of my skin. My very good friend Art Carter barely escaped with his To-Go box of WonderWaffles but did need to get his spinal cord, kidneys, and 90% of his blood replaced.

I have always thought that forgiveness is half empathy and half not having any good ideas for a swift and blinding revenge. And, although we might feel sorry for Mary and her imaginary enemies, feel sorrier for Art Carter and me who have just acquired a new and terrifying real enemy. The thing I fear the most is real and it has a name. Terror, your name is Mary Christmas!

Chapter 1
Mr. Bunny and Mr. Duck's Big Day

Mr. Bunny was a bunny rabbit. He had big floppy ears and a little button nose and crapped little tiny things that looked just a bit like raisins. Mr. Duck was also a bunny except for the fact that Mr. Duck had a species-change operation to make him a Red-butted Orangutan. But this operation went tragically wrong, leaving him ironically deformed to resemble a duck. So the doctors cut off his pinky toe just to prove they were serious when they told him to keep his mouth shut about the whole thing.

One day, Mr. Bunny came over to Mr. Duck's single-wide trailer. "Hey, Mr. Duck, let's take your pet cat, Mr. Cat, for a walk in the park." Mr. Duck informed Mr. Bunny that just because his pet cat was a cat, didn't mean that the cat's name was Mr. Cat, but it was. Now it's been said that a cat has three names. The name you and I call him, the name other cats call him and the name Senior Fuentes. So Mr. Bunny, Mr. Duck, and his pet cat, Mr. Cat (Senior Fuentes), set out for a walk in the park. On the way there, Mr. Bunny saw something on the ground. It looked like a paste or a foam of some kind. The three of them wondered what it could be.

Mr. Bunny, being a bunny of very little brain and even less oral hygiene, thought that the best way to find out what the foam or paste was was to lick it. So he licked and licked and licked some more. He licked so much that Mr. Duck and Mr. Cat became embarrassed about the entire thing. "You should get a room," said Mr. Duck, but it was too late. Mr. Bunny had already dropped his pants.

It seems that Mr. Bunny was loopy on the foam and, sadly, pants-less. Then, Mr. Bunny took off running. When Mr. Duck and Mr. Cat caught up with Mr. Bunny he was buying a couple rocks of crack. But Mr. Bunny couldn't pay the nice crack man. Mr. Crackman then told Mr. Bunny that he better pay up or he would take him to the crack house named Mr. House, and make Mr. Bunny the crack-house bitch.

Mr. Duck, having been a crack-house bitch once before back in the late 80's, gladly paid Mr. Crack the money and left. Some time later, they met Mr. Heroin and Mr. Gallon of Vodka. The Three of them some days later woke up in a pool of their own vomit and urine. Sadly, they never found out what the foam was.

DING!

Chapter I
Stop Calling Me Ishmael

Call me Ishmael. But we both knew Ishmael wouldn't call. In part, because Ishmael didn't have a phone, but mostly because Ishmael was the severely retarded kid who lived down the block.

The Magnificent Captain Pantsdown's super powers were two-fold. Of course the pants-down super power, but, more surprisingly, Ishmael had another power which was hidden until he became Cap'n Pantsdown. And that's about enough on that subject.

DING!

Chapter 1
And the Fur Suit of Happiness

As far as hungry cougars are concerned, humans all taste just a bit like chicken. Some people more than others, but nonetheless, all just a little bit. The other night a group of lightly-intelligent, and, I'm told, chicken-flavored protestors gathered outside my house. They were there to protest me having a good night sleep. They chanted slogans like, "Hell no, we don't have a clue!" "We don't have to work tomorrow!" and "Road work ahead ½ mile". The protests went on until all hours.

The time came for me to act. And act I did. First, I acted out the part from STAR WARS™ where Luke and the Princess swing across the chasm on that rope thing. Then I acted like a freight train run off the tracks in Pissed-offville, Pennsylvania. I tried reasoning with the protestors, but they were far too stupid and un-bathed for that.

"Do any of you know how lucky you are to live in a country where you can walk the streets without fear of oppression? A country where you are free to say what's on your mind, and I'm free to hum a little tune in my head while you do it? Exercise your rights to free speech, but respect my right to come over there and shut you the hell up. We all share a country where being stupid is not a crime but evidently beating some sense into someone who desperately needs it with a tire iron is. A nation where you can peacefully protest in the streets and feel safe knowing that I am saving up my ammunition for Y2K instead of wasting it on your punk-asses now. No more talk; it's smashin' time!"

In an effort to peacefully disperse the crowd, I lobbed no less than eleven opened cans of tuna fish and two pounds of smoked bacon into the crowd and released the cougars. Problem solved.

You know, it's like my father use to tell me. He would say, "Son, it's better to keep your mouth shut and be thought a fool, than to have me come over there and shut it for you." Or even more appropriately, my grandfather would tell me, "Damn-it boy, talk is cheap, but an ass-kickin' comes with a money back guarantee."

Chapter 1

So, evidently, the powers-that-be have made a few changes to the Miranda rights. The changes are, "You have the right to an attorney. If you cannot afford an attorney, then you probably should have thought about that before you decided to break the law. You also have the right to some cake. If you don't like cake, you have the right to a kick in the balls and a shot of pepper spray in the eyes." I always have a hard time choosing, because, Lord help me, I love that spicy stuff.

In an effort to test the legal soundness of the new Miranda ruling, Professor Mojo conducted an experiment. As you recall, Professor Mojo teaches the class "Urban Riot Control Using Cougars 101" at the local community college. He also teaches "Applied Molecular Spanish" and "Quantum Wood Shop". The experiment, however, went horribly wrong. The police said something about "arson" and "thirty nuns trapped inside." It seems that this fire was particularly hot because of all the wooden rulers inside. Professor Mojo can't remember much about that evening due in part to the massive beating he took at the hands of some ruler-toting nuns who escaped the blaze. His knuckles are still swollen and bruised.

The Professor asked me to assemble his legal team. The team consisted of one common house cat, a bath tub filled with cold water, and his Jewish lawyer, Morty Lickschitz. Morty, being a very crafty lawyer, let the house cat and tub of water handle the opening statements. The opening statement began with Morty plunging the cat into the tub of water followed by a five hundred page descriptive analysis of Morty's scrotum and the region just below he called "the sweet spot." The rest pretty much took care of itself. Much to my surprise, Professor Mojo never got his cake and the judge declared a "freakin' mistrial" and quickly cleared the courtroom.

I think the excessive use of a wet cat as a legal defense might have been the wrong thing to do. But Morty insists that it was to prove a point. Not only is justice blind but it's stupid and answers to the name Senior Fuentes. And, sometimes smells like a wet cat. But fairness should be passed out like condoms at a public high school regardless of whether or not the kid even has a chance of getting any action. Human rights should be wielded like a child wields a stick with dog poop on it, indiscriminant of whom it is smeared upon.

Chapter I
'Tis Better to Give then Receive

I have always thought that giving is horribly overrated. The only exception to this is of course "the finger." But if you look at giving like karma, then it takes on an entirely new terrifying dimension. To illustrate this, I will remind you of my very good friend Cap'n Pantsdown. As you recall, Cap'n Pantsdown enjoyed spreading cheer in his own "unique" pant-less way. One day, on his way home from sharing his gift with others, Cap'n Pantsdown was mauled by a bear, which smelled a bit like tacos, just outside the Magic Sandwich™ House of Pasta.

Horrified onlookers tried to comfort each other by giving hugs to the more traumatized people, mostly children and the elderly. But the terror quickly turned to bemusement and annoyance with the distraction. The manager of the Magic Sandwich™ House of Pasta, Archduke Mannheim Monsterplough III, gave Cap'n Pantsdown a mop and 30 minutes to clean up his mess before he called the cops. Yes, it seems that everyone was in a giving mood that day.

Cap'n Pantsdown tried to mop up his mess, but, alas, the lower part of his body was not working very well due in part to his severed spinal cord. The problem was compounded by the fact that his head wound would just not stop bleeding. After the 30 minutes expired, the police escorted Cap'n Pants-

Pantsdown to the maximum brutality prison known as "Candy Land." There, he would live out the rest of his years repaying his debt to society as an aroma therapist for rapists and murders.

Later that same evening, Arch Duke Mannheim Monster-plough III was robbed at gunpoint by someone wearing a bear costume and smelling just a bit like tacos. And oddly enough, everyone who witnessed the brutal mauling that faithful day, within a year's time, was either mauled by a bear or robbed at gunpoint by someone smelling a bit like tacos. We think it is the same bear or maybe a gang of costumed bears that call themselves "Friends of Barbara Bush."

Details are sketchy.

Chapter I
The Twelve Labors of Percules

I never eat the deli chicken. It's chock full of sulfides and sodium; my God, the sodium! Once, my very good friend Art Carter and I were having lunch down on the waterfront so we could watch the whores shoot up and homeless people pee on themselves. Art Carter, despite my warning, got the deli chicken. Sure, it tastes good, but when the glands in his throat started to swell up like a ripe tomato and cut off his breathing, I don't have to tell you, he started to rethink his choice. After no less than seven anti-histamines and four minutes without oxygen to his brain, it was time to go back to work.

On our way back, we passed our very good friend Percules working at his espresso cart. As you recall, Percules was born of the gods but got demoted to human because he abused the phone privileges. We know him now as the mortal Percules, the man who makes the strongest cup of coffee in the world.

As it turns out, Percules was having a bad day. The manager of the espresso cart, Eugene, first commanded him to bring the skin of a terrible pigeon, Senior Fuentes, which was terrorizing the customers. Percules chased the pigeon into an empty polystyrene foam cup and smushed it with his mighty Doc Martin low-top combat shoe.

Next, he was to remove Chief Ten Beers from the table so customers could sit there. The odor was difficult to overcome. As soon as Percules defeated one odor, two more odors would appear. He finally defeated Chief Ten Beers by giving him a dollar and asking him to leave.

With a new found feeling of power surging through him, Eugene then commanded Percules to go get him some lunch at the deli. Armed with only five dollars and one punch card to protect him, Percules made his way to the counter and bravely ordered the six-legged Sulfide Sodium Chicken and brought the breaded pieces back to Eugene.

Chapter I
The Chicken Flavored Universe

The noted physicist, Dr. Phan E. Schlapentickle, once told me that the common expression that "you only get out of it what you put into it" is a gross exaggeration. "You get slightly less out of it than what you put into it, depending on the ambient room temperature." Not only is this an entropic truth, but as he tells it, "Nature's way of saying you can't win, so don't even bother." Truer words have never been spoken.

Dr. Schlapentickle has also been working on a grand unification theory with the help of my very good friend Art Carter. As you recall, Art Carter formulated his own grand unification theory after being severely bitch-slapped by a large, hairy arm-pitted lesbian when he explained his other theory that all energy in the universe, at one time, was located in his penis.

The theory was that "all matter in the universe can be quantified on a singular scale. You and I and everything around us, tastes, more or less, a bit like chicken... Chicken, of course tasting the most like chicken. If we represent chicken as zero on the scale, things tasting less like chicken will be represented by a regressively negative integer. Energy, being very hard to taste, would be represented as a positive integer. Anti-matter and anti-energy would be mathematically opposite of the non-anti-matter and non-anti-energy, possibly being represented by some kind of anti-chicken. It is mathematically possible that there could be some kind of quantum-anti-energy that would taste nothing like anti-chicken at all. It could be represented by a positive integer thus, completing the endless cycle." How simple it all seemed to be.

Now, after no less than five beers each, Dr. Schlapentickle and Art Carter have constructed a theory using both the "Chicken-flavored Universe" theory and the "Law of Entropy," which in a nutshell states that "the more you don't understand something, the less you have to be confused about."

Chapter I
Hey Hugh Get Off of McCloud

As it turns out, my very good friend Art Carter fell victim to the latest wave of corporate layoffs at Global-Corp-Comm-Co. Ltd. Int. Inc. Group, world's fifth largest producer of assembly documentation, corporate memos and production part numbers. The company enlisted the help of the private consulting firm, Layoff-Tech, which was formerly the Law firm of Browne, Brown, Bräun and Fuentes, headquartered in Dogcrap, Missouri. Layoff-Tech specializes in conducting corporate layoffs, company picnics, and Christmas office parties. It seems that Art Carter could in fact be replaced by 17 monkeys each with a typewriter and a bottle of vodka.

Now, Art Carter, believing that there is a divine plan to the universe, that everything happens for a greater purpose, promptly toilet-papered the house of CEO Larry Pasetworth.

Chapter l

My very good friend, Art Carter just got hired to assemble corrugated cardboard boxes for Pandora's Shipping Supply Company. The other day he got an order for box number e1438-90013, the long and flat one with the slotted inserts. As it turns out, the box design had been changed and the existing assembly documentation was tragically obsolete.

Chapter I
Show Me the Monkey

Some have said that the greatest form of love is the love for yourself. Others claim that the greatest form of love is love for others or love for humanity. After ten years of research, scientists at the BurgerTech Research Center have found that the greatest form of love is, in fact, "hot monkey love." Consequently, after this announcement, every monkey shop in town was sold out. The most popular was, of course, the Biter Monkey. But surprisingly, the Red-assed Variegated Vomit Lemur was in ample supply.

The ensuing riots crippled the city for 18 months. The price of a single monkey skyrocketed to an astronomical $1.79. In a frantic attempt to control prices, the government tapped into its strategic monkey reserves and flooded the market with high-quality, low cost government monkeys. The International Consortium of Monkey Producing Nations (ICMPN), countered this move by drastically reducing monkey production and exporting.

Senior Fuentes, spokesman from BurgerTech later confessed that the announcement was a hoax to artificially drive up the price of monkeys. It turns out that BurgerTech is a majority share holder in Pandora's Shipping Supply Co., which is in the process of a hostile take-over attempt of Global-Corp-Comm-Co. Ltd. Int. Inc. Group, also known as the Global Group. As you recall, the Global Group has laid-off 73% of its workforce, all of whom were replaced by 17 monkeys each with a typewriter and a bottle of vodka. The layoffs were an attempt by Global Corp. to reduce operating costs to free up some capital to continue development of its new high-tech "Smart-Bra."

This Smart-Bra is actually a device consisting of advanced polymers, synthetic "reactive" fibers, and a computer chip to automatically control the firmness, support, and cup shape. I don't know how "smart" this bra is, but if it gets to hold and squeeze women's breasts all day, I think it's a very "Lucky-Bra."

Chapter 1
Missouri Loves Company

Dr. Sakana finally maneuvered the school of flesh-eating Attack Trout into a symmetrical shape resembling the face of Alex Trebek. Only problem was Alex looked pissed. Ichthyology had always been the doctor's passion, but this time it looked like he had gone too far. My very good friend Art Carter and I could only look on in horror as the giant face of Alex Trebek, made entirely out of trout, began chewing on the steel bars of the holding tank.

As you recall, ten years previous, Dr. Sakana had been researching UFO sightings over the desert wastelands of Missouri. He discovered that the UFO was in fact haunted by the cross-dressing lesbian ghost of Martha Stewart's estranged gardener, Fernando. It seems that Fernando had been using this haunted UFO to mark the way for the invasion from the planet Gamma-14, inhabited entirely by cross-dressing lesbian gardener ghosts.

One year previous, the citizens of Dogcrap, Missouri, had noticed that strange circles and patterns made out of trout had appeared in the middle of the desert wastelands. These so called "Trout Circles," as the media dubbed them, baffled the authorities for one full year until Dr. Sakana, some meddling teenagers in a groovy van, and a large talking dog solved the mystery. The trout circles held the hidden message to the impending invasion. Enraged that the meddling teenagers and the talking dog got all the credit, not to mention an animated Saturday morning show and subsequent feature film, Dr. Sakana swore revenge.

Knowing full well that no steel holding tank could contain the terrifying face of Alex Trebek, Art Carter and I armed ourselves with lemon juice, tartar sauce, and a side of coleslaw. At that very moment, the door burst open and in rushed some meddling kids and a big talking dog. They walked over to Dr. Sakana and removed the mask. "That's not Dr. Sakana! It's Fernando the gardener! Zoinks!" The big talking dog and a scruffy looking teenager—who, by the way, smelled a lot like a my high school art teacher--ate our coleslaw and a big bucket of something that smelled like soup but turned out to be laundry. Zoinks!

Chapter I
Freaked Out Frankenstein Monsters

That's right, you heard me! My very good friend Art Carter has just subscribed to the latest Cable TV service. It's called the Kill, Kill, Kill Channel.

It's a channel dedicated to 24 hours of freaked-out Bionic Frankenstein monsters programmed to kill, kill, kill all the stupid-ass punk drivers.

The first movie we watched was called, Stupid Assed Punk Drivers and the Freaked-out Bionic Frankenstein Monsters. It was pretty good, but it didn't have enough vampires in it. I found out later that my very good friend Art Carter turned down a subscription to the Genetically Enhanced Cyborg-Vampire Channel, because it didn't have enough movies about Frankenstein monsters killing punk-assed stupid drivers. It did however have plenty of movies about cyborg-vampires eating the guts out of donkey asses. Mmm, that's good-watchin'.

Chapter I

Four years ago, the senator from Utah sponsored a bill eliminating campaigning and elections altogether, except in the case of an evil super-computer taking over the world and killing all the politicians. The bill also included a 300% pay increase and something about a $5 billion tax break for the Special Interest Group's "Soft Money Fund." In the Senator's own words, "It has been made clear to me that the voters know exactly who they want in office. Any further elections would be an insult to the people of this great nation. Forcing the people to endure endless elections, vote after vote, every few years is not in the public interest, and I for one will not stand for it. It is our duty to represent the wishes of the people who elected us and eliminate elections now."

Shortly after the law was passed, the people of this great nation systematically hunted down and skinned every politician whose name appeared on the bill. As it turns out, it was a unanimous vote. The remains of the government, which consisted of the janitor and the guy that ran the copier in the mailroom, enacted legislation to develop a completely computerized government. The computer, <u>Senator-5</u>, went online March 15, 2002.

Chapter I

Much to-do has been made in the media over the return of our home town sports hero, Frampton K. Turdburgler, Jr. As you remember Frampton played lead-off monkey polisher for our local team, the SuckerFish. During the off-season, Turdburgler was approached by Senior Fuentes, the zillionaire owner of our arch-rival team, the Vaginal Discharges, out of Asswater, Texas. Frampton was offered, what would turn out to be the largest contract in the history of professional Greco-Roman Monkey Twisting. His salary was in excess of 2.2 million dollars per foot pound of torque. With an option for additional sandwich bonuses for total monkeys twisted and monkeys extracted from their space suit and jetpacks. The contract itself, was way out of control inasmuch as it was considered seventh largest economic country and responsible for consuming 37% of the world's natural resources and space suit clad monkeys.

The local fans, who once thought him a hero, now booed and jeered him and only purchased his personally endorsed jetpacks and self boosting robotic underpants with contempt and credit cards.

Chapter I
He'll Half Know Furry

Fifteen minutes outside of Leghumpin, Arkansas, my very good friend Art Carter, myself, and a dog named Captain Bitch Master attempted to pass a slow-moving automobile. The automobile was occupied by a small, ill-tempered woman who just happened to be the driver. Our efforts were rewarded with an elevated central finger directed in our general location. In compliance with the newly-ratified 1983 Tokyo Agreement, which clearly states our response "must include but not be limited to either bared ass pressed up against rear window or obscene gesture using tongue and two or more finger of either but not both hands..."

As my very good friend Art Carter began to unbuckle his belt in compliance with the newly-ratified 1983 Tokyo Agreement, I was reminded of the tragic "1982 Tokyo Public Ass-Whoopin' incident," an incident in which the entire nation witnessed a televised broadcast of my very good friend Art Carter receiving a good old fashion roadside ass-whoopin' after cutting off someone in traffic.

I reminded him that on any given day there are 40,000,000 drivers armed with automatic weapons and/or attack cougars, 50% of whom are women. Of the 20,000,000 women armed with automatic weapons and attack cougars, most of them hate men, Art Carter in particular. As reported by Crazy Armed Bitch Magazine, 70% of these women have dissatisfying or unrewarding sex with their partner, all of whom blame Art Carter. According to The National Institute of Health, 22% of armed, angry, sexually-dissatisfied women have considered hunting down and killing my very good friend Art Carter for sport. On any given day, 1 out of 28 are having the worst day of their period. Statistically, on average, every state in the USA has 17,000 square miles of permafrost, including Hawaii.

After hearing the odds, my very good friend Art Carter rebuckled his belt, opened another bottle of vodka, lit a cigar, and continued eating his triple order of Bacon-chili-fries. You see my very good friend Art Carter was painfully aware of the statistic that 1 out of 5 people living in this country will develop heart disease and felt he liked those odds much better.

Chapter I
God, Shave the Queen

After eighteen months of consistently applying the ointment, my very good friend D'Artagnan's rash began to fade. It is important to note that if you forget to apply the ointment one time, the rash comes back like a bowl of chili during an important business meeting.

As you remember, D'Artagnan's rash appeared shortly after he arrived in Hawaii. The circumstances of the appearance of the rash are quite suspicious. It turns out that D'Artagnan had decoded the real meaning of Aloha and the local Hawaiians were pissed. More pissed than usual.

D'Artagnan was working in Hawaii as an openly homosexual activities coordinator for the men's only chartering brokerage, Action Packers. During his training program, "Resentful Indifference and a Hula skirt: a Guide to Hawaiian Hospitality," D'Artagnan noticed that the manual was printed on stationery from a Las Vegas casino. After further research, D'Artagnan had stumbled upon the shocking truth.

Wouldn't you know? Hawaii was not really a chain of volcanic islands located in the middle of the Pacific Ocean! They were, in fact, constructed 22 miles off the coast of California by wealthy casino owner and medicated topical ointment mogul, Senior Fuentes. The islands are actually the landfill debris from Senior Fuentes' massive topical ointment mine located just outside the Las Vegas city limits.

Senior Fuentes, being a shrewd businessman, employed illegal Canadian immigrants and ignorant openly-homosexual activities coordinators to work on his "island paradise" in a secret project code named "Aloha." Who would have known that the word Aloha is literally translated from the ancient Polynesian as, "Screw you, mainlander!"

Chapter I

My very good friend Art Carter once told me that for someone as smart as me, their wisdom would be virtually limited. I responded with one of my pearls of wisdom, "It takes one to know one."

As you recall, my latest project at LingoTech, the third largest developer of business-related acronyms, is something we're calling Metric English. It's a standardized "modular" for the language. For example, instead of individual names for items like "ax," it would be a standard "wood-chopper-upper," and "shovel" would be "dirt-digger-upper", or depending which direction, a "dirt-putter-backer." If we break down the modules, it becomes plain and blunt as the brain in my head.

Chapter I

Long ago, my father would tell me, "Son," he would say, "Son, inherent in every relationship, there are just three things at work. In a delicate balance of symbiosis, a ballet, actions played out in an epic poetic drama." Sadly, he would never tell me what these three things were. On the other hand, we would tell me, "Son," he would say, "Son, there is just one thing you need to know if you want to cook bacon to perfection each and every time." As it turns out, the secret was "Bacon." You have to use actual bacon, not Spray-Co. brand spray on bacon flavored foaming smoothener, but my father never actually told me that either. Sadly, I learned this the smoothened way.

My personal favorite is the non-foaming muffin flavored spray-on smoothener, but by sheer luck, it requires 778.26 foot-pounds of torque to remove the open-proof can lid. That's 13.336 foot-pounds of torque more than my hands or any combination of counter smacking and cussing could produce. At one point I even used my most torque producing swear word, "Hand-dipped", which in the past has produced vast amounts of torque, especially when coupled with spray-Co™ brand spray-on CounterSmak™ with non-foaming hand-dipped smoothening action™. My misfortune was spelled boldly with a capital "T" for the lid was ***T***ragically, Extra™ super open-proof with 33% added Muffin-flavorin™ non-opening action.

Chapter I
Son of Orbiting Death Ray Platform, ver.2.0

"Patty Wack bakes a damn fine piece of cake. I know this for a fact, because in my day I've had some good cake, and hers is damn fine. You might argue that her cake is not as fine a piece of cake as it could be. Sure, but damn fine just the same."

The peaceful banter 'tween my very good friend Art Carter and me was abruptly abrupted by the crackle of my interplanetary orbiting death-ray platform detector. Wouldn't you know it: Dr. Nude--AKA the Fabulous Dr. Nude, AKA Dr. Peter Hangnout--had rebuilt his ultimate weapon of world destruction: a monstrous orbiting platform on which is mounted a death-ray. That's why we all call it an "orbiting death-ray platform." But this one came equipped with an army of giant killer robots and an unstoppable luggage rack of ultimate destruction to boot.

As you recall, the Fabulous Dr. Nude had built an orbiting death-ray platform before, but no one took it seriously because it resembled a large urine stained mattress. The urine stain, if you looked very carefully, bore the likeness of Jesus. So, you know, how threatened would you feel? Another flaw, as it turns out, was that the first version of Dr. Nude's death-ray was also equipped with a Boogie setting and not a very convincing boogie if you ask me. Blah, blah, blah, it fell from the sky in a fiery crash. Problem solved. Or was it?

As it turns out, since the time the orbiting death-ray platform fell from the sky, Dr. Nude had been plotting his revenge. Plotting his revenge and working the drive-up window at the local Burgermonster™ restaurant for $4.75 an hour. One time, I thought I saw him there, working the drive-up window, but figured that it was probably just that leaky exhaust pipe talking again. Besides, do you have any idea how long it would take to save enough money to build another orbiting death-ray platform at $4.75 an hour? But as fate would have it, The Fabulous Dr. Nude must have gotten a raise. He was always pretty good with people. It turns out that later, the management of Burgermonster™ Inc., a subsidiary of SprayCo™ Chicken-flavored Synthetic Polymers, Inc., fired all human drive-up window employees and replaced them with highly-trained Ninja Monkeys to help cut payroll costs. A move which I thought was prudent, considering the economy at the time. The service suffered at first, but once the Ninja Monkeys formed a labor union to improve working conditions, it was fast and friendly every time.

You see, the economy had taken a downturn due in part to the Sixteen Year War which was still raging between the forces of the supreme overlord and a race of super-intelligent, genetically-enhanced dog-men. The super-intelligent, genetically-enhanced dog-men were developed by the BurgerTech Research Center to test the ultimateness of the ultimate double bacon cheeseburger they had been working on over the past five years. The dog-men organized a bloody coup and broke their chains of oppression: a day which will live in infamy, unless you were one of the researchers killed in the violence, at which point you just want to forget the whole thing. The dog-men, along with the dog-women, some of whom I dated, organized a mighty army sworn to destroy all of mankind, including the evil genius, Dr. Geoff (pronounced Dr. Roger). Now, having someone sworn to destroy you, not to mention an entire race of dog-men, didn't sit well with Dr. Geoff (Dr. Roger) and he blamed that on mankind. So, as a form of revenge, he took matters into his own hands and vowed to destroy mankind before the dog-men got to him.

Five years earlier, Dr. Geoff (Dr. Roger), had been taking "Evil Genius" lessons from Commander Nick Knack, Patty Wack's common law husband and noted local evil genius and aroma therapist. On his way to Commander Knack's office, Dr. Geoff (Dr. Roger), who at the time was only a nurse, cut someone off in traffic. Sure, some fingers where raised and harsh words exchanged, but it was all in fun. Well, it's fun until someone vows to destroy you and all of mankind for cutting you off in traffic. The man who was cut off in traffic was none other than Rich Richmanson, stepson of Manfred Manfieldson, the local authority on anti-giant killer robot targeting systems and pie and self proclaimed "one sexy bitch". One thing that Rich Richmanson did quite often was vow to destroy you and the rest of mankind, but he was mostly full of crap. But Nurse Geoff, (pronounced Senior Fuentes) took this threat very seriously. Nurse Geoff (Roger) knew that Rich Richmanson's father, Manfred Manfieldson, was an expert at building anti-giant killer robot systems. So, Nurse Geoff (nurse), needed to develop some kind of offensive defense to offend against Richmanson's defenses. The logical offensive defense was to build an army of giant killer robots. Blah, blah, blah, a few years later, Rich Richmanson cracked under the stress and is now the local authority on wandering the streets aimlessly, mumbling things under his breath. But convinced that it was a good idea, the now Dr. Geoff (doctor), continues to develop his mighty army of giant killer robots, so he can loose them on mankind.

Quickly, my very good friend Art Carter and I made it to

our jet-powered robotic attack armor, ready to do battle with the Fabulous Dr. Nude and his new orbiting death-ray platform. But Art Carter had locked his keys inside. Aside from ending sentences with a preposition, that was something Art Carter was renowned for. Faced with this new dilemma, we both quickly reasoned that the Fabulous Dr. Nude wasn't doing anything wrong, so we didn't have to leave yet. He had just built an orbiting death-ray platform. There wasn't any law against that. At least not yet...

Four year previously, a bill was introduced into congress which would make the manufacturing, possession of or trafficking in orbiting death-ray platforms illegal if the purpose was to destroy mankind. But the Senator from Utah attached a rider to the bill and it got bogged down and later killed in the Senate because of the dairy subsidies. Ironically, the Senator from Utah was none other than Patrick McGroin. As you recall, Pat McGroin was elected on the campaign platform that if you reduce the human body down to its chemical elements, it's worth $1.26. But Pat McGroin had swallowed a nickel as a child which never passed, so if we reduce him down to his chemical elements, he was worth $1.31. Not surprisingly, he defeated his opponent by a landslide. His opponent was none other than my very good friend Art Carter and his freakishly huge penis. But that, being neither here nor there, was completely irrelevant. All that mattered now was that this looked to be some kind of government conspiracy, and government conspiracies aren't illegal. At least not yet...

Later that evening, after no less than nine beers each, my very good friend Art Carter and I finished our first draft of what we hoped would someday be a new law, a law that would ban orbiting death-ray platforms, government conspiracies, and fat chicks wearing tight pants in public. It would also make "Purple Haze" the national anthem and bacony our national odor. All we needed now was someone to check for spelling errors and margins. That man was none other than my dear old grandpa. Grandpa was happily living out his years in the maximum security prison known as "Senior Fuentes." But we had other plans for him. You see Grandpa had a real problem with his temper. He had an even bigger problem with tax collectors and shooting at them, but was an excellent speller and not bad with margins. One day, after Grandpa spent no less than 16 hours laying fiberglass in an unventilated basement, the local tax collector, Dick Head, came over to wish Grandpa a happy "Pay your back taxes day." Still loopy from the fumes, Grandpa put 177 rounds of Russian made 7.62's into the tax collector,s back. To this day he insists that it was in self-defense. "The first shot spun 'im 'round and dropped the bastard. So I figured, empty all six magazines into 'im. Oh yeah, he came at me with a knife." My grandpa use to tell me, "Damn-it boy, why the hell you gotta go dressin' up like a girl?" He would also tell me, "Damn-it boy, if you gonna do something, go way the hell overboard." So, the hell overboard we went.

Even later that same evening, my very good friend Art Carter and I arrived at the maximum security prison, known as "Candy Land," dressed in our disguises and fully "loaded." I was disguised as a man wearing all black clothes and black shoe polish on my face. Art Carter was disguised as Art Carter. You see, through a strange turn of events and some embarrassing newspaper headlines in the wake of his senatorial run, it turns out that the most popular Halloween costume for the past five years has been dressing up as my very good friend Art Carter. But that's neither here nor there. With all the stealth and skill of a card carrying member of Ninja Monkeys Local #107, we snuck to the main guard tower and asked the attendants if we could see my grandpa. After about thirty bucks each, the guards agreed to allow me in, but informed us that, through an act of congress, this was an "Art Carter Free Zone," so my freaky friend had to wait in the car. And wait in the car he did.

I quietly crept through the hallways of the prison until a guard stopped me. "What he heck are you s'pose to be?" Shocked that I had been spotted with such a clever disguise, I blurted out the first thing that came to mind. "Shhh, someone will hear you." I motioned for the guard to come closer as if I had a secret for him. Just as the guard lent me his ear to hear the "secret," I gave him such a Kung-fu chop on the neck. But this guard must have had a Kung-fu resistant neck because he just looked at me and let loose with his mighty, prisoner-smacking stick. I have to admit, he was quite skilled, and it felt good to see all those tax dollars go for such superior training.

Three weeks later, on my way home from the hospital, I ran into my very good friend Chief Ten Beers and his invisible friend, Mutha Fugger. Now, I have never seen Mutha Fugger, but I have smelled him, and the Chief talks to him all the time. As it turns out, Mutha Fugger had done something very bad, and Chief Ten Beers was scolding him. "Why'd you go and do that, Mutha Fugger?" He said. Mutha Fugger was characteristically silent. "You stupid, Mutha Fugger?" Again no reply. "Ahhh, shi' man, who'da Mutha Fugger did this?" After a few minutes of listening to the conversation, I deduced that someone had wet Chief Ten Beers pants, and I think Mutha Fugger did it. I asked if there was anything I could do to help, but as I did, a far less invisible friend showed up. It was Cap'n Fromwell, the local police lieutenant. Cap'n Fromwell asked me if Chief Ten Beers was bothering me. I looked at Cap'n Fromwell with my standard look of confusion. Chief Ten Beers responded by saying "No, no, no, Mutha Fugger botherin' me." At that very moment, I looked up to see Dr. Nude's death-ray platform hanging low off the horizon far in the distance. I looked back at Cap'n Fromwell, this time with fear in my eyes and said, "He's gotta be stopped!" Cap'n Fromwell turned and tackled Chief Ten Beers and I am assuming Mutha Fugger as well. Which was all well and good because that Mutha Fugger seemed to be a trouble maker.

Chapter I

"Call me Ishmael." But I don't think Ishmael is gonna call. We all know someone like Ishmael. Ishmael is the severely retarded kid who lives just down the street. His life is a wonderful, moment-to-moment adventure filled with small personal victories every day. Things that we take for granted like "getting it in the toilet" and "remembering pants" are triumphant symbols of accomplishment for Ishmael. Sometimes I wish I could be as lucky as Ishmael. Everybody is very supportive of him. "Way to play ball, sport!" We also like to laugh at the severely retarded kid, because he doesn't know what was going on so, no harm done. Sometimes people treat me like they treat Ishmael. I will explain something I accomplished, or a small personal victory, and I get the same response that Ishmael would get. "Oh, that's just wonderful!" or "Super job, champ!" I remember once as a child, I built a television out of a coat hanger, some paperclips, tin foil and an empty mayonnaise jar. This device would broadcast as well as receive television signals. It got its power from the RF electricity I had been transmitting via the two hundred foot tall Tesla coil I built in the back yard out of a 1965 Buick Electra and some speaker wire. The Tesla coil had caused some kind of reaction with the ionosphere and solar radiation, creating a harmless, self-sustaining plasma field in our atmosphere eliminating the need for external electrical power. All I got was a "nice work, slugger!" So I took apart the entire thing, and the military confiscated my notebooks and shipped me to a new city to live out my life with my new parents.

Chapter I

My very good friend Art Carter insists that "life is like a bucket." The bucket is empty but it can be filled with whatever you want. My father would tell me, "Son, when life hands you lemons, put the lemons in a box filled with scorpions and mail 'em back to the bastard." I, however, feel that life is like a car's glove compartment, you spend years cramming it full of napkins, warranties and other useless junk until finally it is so cram-packed with crap you just have to abandon it behind the old warehouse down by the train tracks. Many nights my very good friend Art Carter and I would talk about this very subject. We would also talk about Caledonia, the long-legged cheerleader from high school. Turns out that she was dating an older college guy, so I never really had a chance. Or did I? For having as troubled a past as he did, my very good friend Art Carter is a wealth of wisdom. Much as Chief Ten Beers spews forth vomit and urine, so too does Art Carter spew revelations of truth. Not a day would go by without Art Carter enlightening me with some kernel of philosophy. Things like, "Pat it with a damp towel, or you'll just rub the stain in," and "If you pick it, it will never heal." We all called Art Carter's dad "Papa Carter," but Art would call him "Uncle Daddy." Now, this would enrage Uncle Daddy, not only because it was true, but because Art Carter was the illegitimate bastard son of his sister's ex-boyfriend, a mysterious man she called "Senior Fuentes." Papa Carter would always call Art Carter, "Get over here, Bastard!" He had other cute nicknames for him like, “Where the hell's that beer boy?” and “I'm gonna count to three.” Funny, he would say, “I'm gonna count to three,” but then end up calling him “One, two, damn-it now!” Once, Art Carter's brothers, Gilgamesh and Agamemnon, who were not only twins, but evil as well, sold him into slavery. You see, they were jealous of Art Carter's new multi-colored jacket. Not just the jacket, but as Gilgamesh tells it, “There was other stuff too.” After seven years of forced servitude, Art Carter had developed a mighty legion of giant killer robots he playfully named Deathcom-destructobots. The giant killer robots could change from the shape of a giant killer robot into a far less useful form. An example of this was the head robot, Mega-decepta-transformo-gorobo-transa-forma-tron, who could change into a harmless looking hotdog vending cart. Although useful for deception, a hotdog vending cart was not a worthy adversary in battle. These design flaws where brought painfully to light during test battle simulations when Mega-decepta-transformo-gorobo-transa-forma-tron was crushed by another giant killer robot known as “Smash-bot.”

Many years passed. Art Carter had redesigned his giant killer robots, not so much because the idea was flawed, but because it came dangerously close to infringing on Marvel Comics™ copyrights. With the help of the re-designed giant killer robots, Art Carter had captured most of the southern hemisphere and a large part of Utah. He ruled with an iron fist, smashing his enemies with his mighty legion of Non-Transforming™ giant killer robots. The time came for all of his subjects to make a pilgrimage and pay homage to the mighty Art Carter, who, at this time, had changed his name to Dirty Sanchez to impress the chicks. His two evil twin brothers, Gilgamesh and Agamemnon, approached the mighty Dirty Sanchez, horrified to see that it was their brother. The Marquee quickly recognized Gilgamesh and Agamemnon, who had sold him into slavery so many years ago, and sentenced them to be imprisoned in the spankotron chamber for a seven-year spankin'. Gilgamesh and Agamemnon pleaded for their asses. "Please spare our asses!" they pleaded. The mighty Dirty Sanchez agreed to spare them on one condition. "If you can give me an answer to this riddle, I will not only spare you, but I will hand over my kingdom to you." Art Carter was very confident that his brothers would never be able to answer his riddle. "But if you are wrong, you will live out your years in butt-blistering agony." Dirty Sanchez paused; then, in a quiet and ominous voice he spoke, "What walks on four legs as a child, two legs as an adult and three legs as an old man?" Gilgamesh and Agamemnon, having not just fallen off the turnip wagon, quickly said, "It's Man. You screwed up the whole thing. You suck at this!" They quickly grabbed Art Carter around the neck and noogied him severely. "All right, you all heard the Marquee, we're in charge now." Gilgamesh and Agamemnon ruled the empire for only three weeks. They lost the empire and two hundred bucks in a poker game to Arch Duke Mannheim Monster-plough III. My very good friend Art Carter, having been exiled from his once mighty empire, began to journey northward. North to the northern most city of Milquetoast: a city of opportunity, a land of dreams, a place where the roads were paved with milk and toast. Not the most effective method of road construction, but the citizens of Milquetoast kind of had a motif in mind. The journey to Milquetoast was long and perilous, filled with exciting adventures and great dangers. But none as interesting as the time my very good friend Art Carter, having drunk only six beers to protect him, attempted to run nakedly through a pack of angry lesbians. Of course, mayhem erupted and the police had to hose down the entire crowd with chicken fat and release the hungry police cougars to clear the streets. Ironically, after being beaten by large, hairy arm-pitted women, Art Carter had an epiphany. Art Carter formulated the grand unification theory right off the top of his head that day. “All matter in the universe can be quantified on a singular scale. You and I and everything around us, tastes, more or less, a bit like chicken. Chicken, of course tasting the most like chicken. If we represent chicken as zero on the scale, things tasting less like chicken will represent a regressively negative integer. Not being able to taste it, energy would be represented as a positive integer. Anti-matter and anti-energy would be mathematically opposite of the non-anti-matter and non-anti-energy. Possibly being represented by some kind of anti-chicken.” How simple it all seemed to be.

Chapter I

On his way to the town of Milquetoast, wandering the mountainous region of Vönderbrä, Art Carter came across a curious little man. The man wore his smile like an ass wears a bicycle seat. His clothes were tattered and baggy. On the top of his head he wore a tightly-fitted baseball cap with the inscription, "Guns Make Me Smart." Beneath the cap was long matted hair the color of unfortunate polyester work slacks. His name was Testiclese. Testiclese carried with him a laminated wooden board with four small plastic wheels on the bottom. He would stand on the board and roll down the path. As they were both on their way to Milquetoast, they decided to keep company together on the journey. As they walked down the path through the Vönderbrä Mountains, Testiclese related many of his own stories to Art Carter in his slow, somewhat vacant voice... "January 15, double-knot. As fate would have it, I found myself in the town of Riboflavin, on the banks of the River Senior Fuentes. Confronted by a swarm of genetically-enhanced super bees known as 'penis stingers,' most of which had spent the entire day drinking and listening to depressing redneck country music. The bees desired my fruit pie, but I shan't surrender it to the dudes. The battle raged on, seemingly for hours, until, alas, the fruit pie was completely consumed by yours truly."

Chapter I

I remember once, a long time ago... It was on my way to the coffee shop at the corner. I remember this quite clearly, which is odd in that I rarely remember things that actually happen, and even rarer do I remember those things clearly. This is in part due to my freakishly short attention span and the fact that something probably distracts me from my cocoa with fifteen hundred foot-pounds of torque and a mint on the hood of my eight horsepower, high-topped trousers.

I was going to the coffee house to pick up the latest issue of Containers Digest, the third largest publication dedicated to containing things and the digestion of containment technology.

The cover story was about mint flavored trousers and the things you could, and quite frankly should, contain therein. My curiosity and trousers were peaked due in part to the pointed apex, custom-built into my curiosity, as well as a self-peaking feature I had installed for just a few bucks extra. The self-peaking feature was a free gift with the subscription to Pinnacle Magazine, the magazine dedicated to self-pointing pants. For an additional fifteen hundred dollars you could have a magnetic point installed in the apex of your pants, which would allow you to always point at Magnetic North, or 22 degrees Northeast for those of us living in or around the Greater Seattle area.

Quite my mistake, I had forgotten to bring my money. Instead, I brought only a pocket can opener and a quite impressive collection of spent gum wrappers and lint. Having the qualities of being both pocket-sized and portable, I more than likely plunged the device deep inside my hand containment apertures built directly into my pants. This too could have contributed to the preponderance of my pantage, and the heretofore mentioned pointage.

The can opener, mostly by chance and actually by squeezing and twisting, was used earlier that morning to extricate soup from its container--a process I had read about, quite by chance and mostly by phonetics and word recognition, (and, yes, a little squeezing and twisting) even earlier that morning in my latest issue of Containers Digest Swimsuit Issue featuring a cover photo of Senior Fuentes and a complete list of the fifty sexiest soups in North America.

Chapter I

It's a well-known fact that, "that which does not destroy you will make you stronger." I personally feel if it doesn't destroy you, you're probably not doing it right.

My grandfather use to tell me, "Damn-it boy, can you tell me why I didn't sell you to the circus folk when they was in town?" He would also tell me, "Damn-it boy, if it don't destroy you, you've gotta hunt it down and kill it with your own bare hands, eat its butt and that's how you absorb its spirit energy. That's what'll make you stronger. Else-wise, it's gonna come back lookin' fer ya, and this time you might not be so lucky."

My very good friend Art Carter would have me believe that, if it doesn't destroy you, it's okay to keep doing it 'til a rash develops, then it's time to stop.

On the other hand, my grandmother espoused a philosophy that went, "If it hasn't killed your grandfather, then the check must not have cleared the bank, and it'll come look'n' for me very soon." I question my grandmother's reliability, though. Not because she carried on long, animated philosophical discussions with rising bread dough; that really didn't bother me. It was her subscription to Reader's Digest that made me suspicious. Her copy had only the odd number pages in it. This was curious in and of itself due in part to the evenhandedness of my grandmother, which rendered her odd pages as useless as a French declaration of war, and the fact that the rising bread dough would whole-wheatedly agree with her opinions.

At first, the idea of having something not destroy you making you stronger sounds as silly as a modern day French military victory. But by means of comparison, food has little destructive power and if eaten can make you stronger. Conversely, drinking three shot glasses of chlorine bleach followed by an after dinner fist-full-o'-sleeping pills would probably not make you stronger, even if you did wake up. Spinal cord removal and pencil-to-the-eye are yet other examples.

I think the greatest example of something not destroying you yet not making you stronger would probably be a hair cut or a gift certificate.

Ka-pudin' and that's how it's done.

Chapter I
I Wanted a Bud Lite

On many occasions, it has come to my attention--and through a painfully long and pointless series of deductions I like to call "cyclical enlightenments"--it has never been said, neither spoken nor written, that God was not a giant spider. And by basic laws of Chaos theory and the Improbability Principle, which states that the more unlikely something is, or is not, to be, the more certain that it is, or is not. This means that scientifically, God could be nothing less than a giant spider.

After much deliberation (and no fewer than ten beers), I have come up with a new interpretation of the Testaments--Old and New. At no time anywhere in the Bible is it written that God was not a giant spider. This is not to say that God could not be some other kind of giant insect or possibly bear or lizard. It does however say many times that we humans were created in His image. This could mean that possibly the markings on the abdomen of the Great Giant Spider God look remarkably and terrifyingly human-shaped. Because I don't look much like a giant lizard or a bear, do I?

My very good friend Art Carter has found reason to believe that the Bible was actually written by and for spiders, and quite by chance that in all the writings of the Bible, the spiders were merely on the shoulders of people, and had gone undetected until now, because it's the will of and pleases the Great Spider God.

I guess he could also be some kind of ant or even a giant caterpillar or something.

My very good friend Art Carter also reasoned, much to everyone's consternation, that Jesus Christ was simply a mathematical genius, brilliant dietician, and a fashion guru. He could also dance like a freak and bowled a 273 game once. Now I don't claim to be a Biblical scholar or bowling expert, but 273 sounds a little far-fetched if you ask me.

Chapter 1

The Grand Opening of the new theme park, Ass World, was met with surprisingly limited enthusiasm, due in large part to the long lines at the "J-lo Ride" and the crippling twenty-five drink minimum. Moments later, the gates exploded, freeing all the imprisoned and illegally imported sex weasels with matching attachments and WhippedTopping® brand Sex-O-Cream topical penis adhesive dispenser.

Sadly, none of the sex Weasels survived, due in no small part to the lack of napkins and the seeping issues inherent in the dispensers' design, and the fact that the explosion also freed thirteen hundred rare and endangered sex falcons, which quickly devoured the weasels in a bloody and vanilla-flavored feeding orgy, whipped to creamy perfection by the frantic biting and clawing of the doomed topical penis-adhesive-ointment-covered weasels.

It was at that very moment I realized that each of us at one point in our lives, comes to one unmistakable moment--not unlike when you lean too far backwards in a chair and your hair or clothing suddenly gets caught in some machinery or caught on fire by something electrical that it might have touched while leaning back in the chair, and just as you realize that your hair or clothes are caught in machinery or on fire, you find out that the chair is in the middle of a lake of boiling hot alligators covered with lava and dynamite and spiders.

And the alligators have been drinking for five or six

hours, and I think the spiders are radioactive too.

That's when you realize that each and every one of us is sadly the product of our upbringing. This point was illustrated crystal clearly just last Wednesday. My very good friend Art Carter had just finished up our jug of Sex-O-Cream spray-on vanilla Sunday topping, when I realized that for the last fifteen years I had ended each and every sentence with the phrase, "For crying out loud!"

I had picked up this phrase from my mother--at a time she calls "in my childhood," but I refer to as "the eighteen years of my life I can't seem to remember, yet I scream in terror when I try to recall it; back before I moved out of my parents' house, for crying out loud."

Chapter 1

Capt'n Fromwell's fabulous dancing poodles performed as expected. The dancing and prancing was without a doubt tantalizing. Many critics have, of recent, found fault in the poodles' performance saying "the prancing about like little doggie ballerinas is top-notch, but the costumes are amateurish at best, and the snacks, don't get me started about the snacks."

Roger (pronounced Chad Swirly), of the Frampton City Times said, "It's hard to imagine a more poorly executed poodle dance if you tried. But if I get super drunk and attach steel tipped nipple clips to my nipples and testicle clamps to my testicles… and then twirl around in some kind of a nipple clipped, testicle clamped drunken stumbling moron pretending to dance like poodles…, well that might come close, but could still be better than Capt'n Fromwell's so called 'poodles'."

Oddly enough, Roger Whisker (Chad Swirly) was the restaurant reviewer. And in sharp contrast to reviewing restaurants and dining, liked to compare almost everything to a drunken nipple clipped, testicle clamped twirling extravaganza!

Unaccustomed to, and grossly ill-equipped for such a clamping review, Capt'n Fromwell put no fewer than seven rounds into the head and torso of each of his so called "fabulous dancing poodles". The end.

Chapter I

My father use to tell me, "Son", he would say, "Just try to keep your fingers outta there." And to this day no truer words have ever been spoken. He would also tell me, "That beer aint gonna drink it-self."

To this day, rarely has his advice failed me, so much so that, it was adopted as the slogan for my company Lingotech. As you remember, Lingotech is the world's 3rd largest of infrared guided rocket powered "Everythingers™" and burst resistant trousers. "Lingotech, just try to keep your fingers outta there."

The company initially tried to market the slogan to international proctology supply companies, but sadly, that joke is even too easy for this book. Lingotech also marketed a slogan to Compu-smooth, the largest manufacturer of Non-clamping, grip-resistant men's undergarments called skid-R-oos, "just try to keep your fingers outta there." After that, Lingotech changed the slogan to "Lingotech, 50 years of selling crap to the stupid."

Chapter I

As I reinitialized the primary boot partition of my computerized self sagging Chocolate Brown slacks with built in bus pass and stealth enhanced "chick-resistant" spray-on Pantz-coating™, the concept finally hit me, hit me like a ton of fat-woman ass on a bus seat. I have to bring more stuff than I can carry in one pair of pants to work with me. I remember a simpler time when all I needed to bring to work was my polyester Chocolate Brown slacks and a real crappy attitude.

Some of the items I bring with me are more for tradition than any actual use. For example a large and expensive laptop computer used exclusively for playing solitaire. This replaces my light and inexpensive deck of cards, and any desire to actually play the game. My briefcase is filled with granola bars and empty zip-o-lock baggies. Some of which have been used only once to harbor a sandwich of constructed of Spray-Co™ spray-on tuna flav-R sandwich spray and some kind of clear oil which might have been mayo.

Along with the afore mentioned I like to bring an extra pair of emergency roll-out underpants™ and a package of Bachelor™ brand CleanShirt™ the prepackaged disposable food (and urine) resistant shirt substitute.

Throughout the day, I try to avoid urine spraying / spattering situations and fortunately for me and many of my coworkers at Lingotech, the world's third largest producer of disgruntled, urine spraying workers, and employees suffering from concussive bowel syndrome, I have only had to use the underpants twice.

Chapter I

Recently my very good friend Art Carter announced his candidacy to the office of President of the Untitled States of America. As you recall, my very good friend Art Carter along with his freakishly huge penis ran for president and vice president, back in 1984 but was defeated by a landslide.

Turns out, on the night of the election, the then senator of Utah, staged a landslide and announced to the public that not only has my very good friend Art Carter been killed in the slide, but his last dying wishes was not to vote for him due in no small part to the ongoing disagreement between him and his freakishly huge penis on domestic policy.

This year's campaign is "Vote for Art Carter because I'm not crushed to death, and I'm not Ralph Nader." He is also withholding his political party affiliation until after the election stating, "Where-ever the votes come from, that's where I go." Art Carter. The Flip-flop candidate.

Foremost and paramount to Art Carter's policies is to improve the economy, reduce traffic and create jobs. And as Art Carter would say, with just two words "Snipers." Highly paid government traffic snipers. The advantages would be three fold.

1. Plenty of overpaid, gun-wielding government workers with lots of money to complain about how small both of their powerboats are and how it's been three years since they bought their last motorcycle and so on.
2. Reduced traffic. If one of every 1000 cars is "sniped",

do you really need to drive anywhere?

3. The policy would open new “sniper” related industries. Sniper Training, Sniper Avoidance training.
4. He also wants to Run under the “No Fat-chicks” platform.

Chapter I

Over the course of the past 45 years, I have tried to maintain what I like to call a degree of "Nuclear Opacity." This is to say that I neither confirm nor deny my own nuclear capabilities.

The policy has proven quite successful on any number of levels including my FREE subscription to "**Possible Threat to Democracy**" magazine and the "**So, you've decided to neither confirm nor deny your nuclear capabilities**" cable channel. Which in and of itself is reason enough, but don't get me started.

Unfortunately, my next-door neighbor Roger Kaleidoscope resists this policy of Nuclear Opacity by bringing his A-bomb out every weekend, weather permitting, and giving it a good washing. Oh, he'll talk it up real good at the local tavern, "My A-bomb" this and "polished glass parking lot that." It really gets old in a hurry, but far be it from me to say anything, because, well he does have an A-bomb you know.

My very good friend Art Carter thinks that this Nuclear Opacity policy, the looming threat of mutually assured destruction coupled with a strict "No Fat Chicks" Doctrine could make all the difference in a confrontation situation. Art Carter would explain, "It would be like 'you want to start something punk? You don't know if I've got nuclear capabilities or not…'" and "wow, she didn't look fat last night."

Printed in the United States
29494LVS00001B/322-333

9 781932 672060